Katy's Box

Katy's Box

Mary Evelyn Notgrass McCurdy

Illustrated by the Author

Notgrass History
Gainesboro, Tennessee
notgrass.com

Text and Illustrations Copyright © 2017
by Mary Evelyn Notgrass McCurdy
Cover Background Images by BK0808 / Shutterstock.com
and Ilya Bolotov / Shutterstock.com

ISBN 978-1-60999-115-9
Printed and Bound in the United States of America

Contents

Dedicated to my parents,
Ray and Charlene Notgrass,
and to John and Bethany, my brother and sister.

Thank you for making me feel loved.

Katy's Box

1

The Box

Katy lay on her back in the grass, trying to be as lazy as she could since it was the last day of summer. The grass tickled her legs and the sun made her squint until her eyes were barely open as she tried to find pictures in the clouds. She saw the shapes of a dragon, a duck, and a canoe.

When she couldn't stand the brightness any more, she closed her eyes. She thought about school the year before. There were some things she would rather forget, like the day one of the class troublemakers spit glue in her face or all the times her teacher had given one of her classmates a sour look. There were some good memories, though, like playing with her friend during recess and finding rolly pollys to take care of together.

Recess would be different this year. Almost everything about school would be different now that her only classmates would be her brother and her sister.

An ant crawled up a dandelion next to Katy's head. She turned to watch him walk gingerly down the other side of the stem. "Were you ever homeschooled?" Katy asked the ant. "Maybe you're homeschooled right now! I wonder how old you are. I'm eight, but I'll be nine in just a few weeks." The ant reached the bottom of the stem and Katy lost sight of him in the grass. Just then she heard the side gate screech open. Her sister Anna walked through the gate with her dog at her side. Once Anna and Sparky were in the back yard, Anna closed the gate and unhooked Sparky's leash. Sparky bolted across the yard toward the playhouse at the back, turned around so fast he fell sideways, and ran straight toward Katy. Katy shielded her face with her arms as Sparky jumped on her and Anna tried unsuccessfully to make him stop.

"Are you sure that's the same dog you picked out at the animal shelter?" Katy asked. "I think they must have made a switch when you weren't looking. Sparky has to be one of the wildest dogs in Urbana, Illinois!"

"He didn't feel good that first day we saw him," Anna replied. "He was waiting for someone to come love him and give him a reason to be happy."

Earlier in the summer, on Anna's eleventh birthday, their parents had surprised her with a trip to the animal shelter where she got to pick her very own dog. It was a dream come true for Anna and she was ecstatic. They looked at several different dogs and Anna really wanted a little female puppy named Belle. Another family had already picked her out, though, and Anna had to decide on a different one. She considered a feisty Pomeranian, but after he bit Dad while they were in the visiting room she thought she should keep looking.

Anna had finally decided on a black and white mutt whom she named Sparky. Sparky had shaggy paws and a scruffy beard. That day at the animal shelter he was calm and quiet and mannerly, but the Porters soon found out these qualities were not Sparky's true character.

After climbing on Katy and giving her left leg a good scratch, Sparky finally ran out of steam and flopped down on the grass between Anna and Katy. Katy rubbed his spotted belly while Anna scratched his head behind his ears.

"It's going to feel strange not walking to school in the morning," Anna said.

"You'll still have to walk down the stairs to the basement!" Katy replied. Anna didn't think her joke was very funny.

"Ha, ha," she said sarcastically. "It's going to be so weird having Mom as the teacher all day."

"It will be kind of strange, but I think I'm excited. No more glue spitting or fire drills or waiting in long lines."

Their dad opened the back door and headed toward the garbage cans at the back of the garage.

"Hi, Dad!" Anna and Katy called out, surprised it was already time for him to be home from work. Dad carried a white cardboard box to the trash can they used for recycling.

"Dad, wait!" Katy called as she ran over to him. "May I have that box, please? I've been wanting one about that size."

"Sure, Honey," Dad said as he handed her the box.

Katy looked at the printing on the top. "Educational Supply Store," she read out loud. "What came in this?" Dad said it was Seth's math book and some flash cards for her. Katy felt a flutter in her stomach. At first she wasn't sure if it was a nervous feeling or an excited one. She decided it was some of both.

Anna followed Dad back inside. Katy sat down in the grass with her empty box, thinking. Anna soon poked her head outside and told Katy it was time to eat. Katy took the box to her room and laid it on the bottom bunk. Her project would have to wait until later.

While the Porters ate their chicken casserole, Mom talked about her plans for their first day of school. She had set up a desk for each of her students in the den and she and Anna had decorated the bulletin board together. Seth's math book and Katy's flash cards were the last of the materials she had ordered for the first semester. She was glad they had arrived in time.

After Katy helped clean up the kitchen, she hurried to her room. She was glad Anna wanted to read on the couch. There were nice things about sharing a room with her sister, but sometimes Katy liked to do things by herself.

"Okay, Sugar Plum," Katy said to the rag doll on her bed. Sometimes she talked to her doll like a friend just for fun. "This box is perfect. I've been wanting one just like it." Katy had seen an old movie a few months before in which a little girl kept a cardboard box under her bed. The box contained the girl's most treasured possessions. Ever since she had seen the movie, Katy had thought about what she would put in a special box if she had one under her own bed. Now that the box was sitting in front of her, she had to rack her brain to come up with things to put in it.

She wanted the contents of the box to remind her of special events as well as everyday happenings. She imagined growing up and showing the box to her husband and children some day. She wondered what they would be interested in seeing. She thought about things her parents had shown her from their childhoods.

Katy liked to see the little stuffed panda her dad had loved when he was a boy. He had loved it until one button eye disappeared and the panda was dirty and floppy. Katy liked to think of what her dad must have been like as a little boy.

Mom always took special care of the little purple and white tea set that she kept on a shelf in her bedroom. Her grandmother had given it to her when she was little. Katy wanted to be able to show her own children things like that someday.

Katy treasured letters she received in the mail and notes people wrote to her. She liked to look back at drawings and paintings she did when she was younger and see how much her skills had improved.

Most of the photos in their house were in their family photo albums, but Katy had a few photos that were her own. One of her favorites was of Seth, Anna, and herself sitting with Irene in Irene's living room. Irene was their special friend from church who was like a grandmother to them.

Katy went to her dresser and opened the jewelry box on top. In the left compartment was a necklace with small white beads that spelled Katy's name. Katy had worn it in a portrait session when she was four. Somehow it had become impossibly tangled, but Katy still kept it in her jewelry box because it was special. The necklace was the first thing Katy put in the cardboard box.

She found the picture with Irene and laid it in the box as well. On a shelf in her closet she found the first journal she ever kept. She put it in the box, along with a painting of a grassy field and a blue sky that was on another shelf in her closet. The painting was nothing grand, but Katy remembered how proud she had been

when she finished it a few years before.

In the bottom of Katy's closet was a basket of old toys. She found the little doll with the pink lacy dress her grandparents gave her when she was three. One of the doll's eyes was missing like her dad's panda. Katy always found it odd that the doll had blue hair. She never played with the little doll anymore, but it was special because her grandparents had given it to her. Katy put the doll in the box on her bed.

Katy also put in a heart-shaped rock she had found at the ocean when she was six and the pink hairbow that matched a dress her mom had made for her. The dress was too small now. The last thing she put inside was an acorn that had been on her dresser since the previous fall when she and Anna had gathered acorns together at their neighbor's house down the street.

Katy looked in her box. There wasn't anything especially beautiful. She knew what she had chosen would not look significant to anyone else, but everything was special to her. The box looked rather empty, but Katy wanted to leave plenty of room, so she was satisfied.

"I'll let that be all for now," Katy said to Sugar Plum. There were two big drawers under the white wooden bunk bed in Anna and Katy's room. Katy pulled out the drawer that was hers and moved things around until she had room for her box in the corner. She pushed the drawer back under the bed with her feet. She hoped at least one special thing would happen during their first year of homeschooling that would give her something else to put in her box.

2

The First Day of School

At 8:30 a.m. on the first day of school in the basement of the Porter's house, Seth, Anna, Katy, and their mom recited together, "I pledge allegiance to the flag of the United States of America and to the Republic for which it stands, one nation under God, indivisible, with liberty and justice for all." They all faced the small American flag Mom had hung on the wall next to the bulletin board. When they were finished, they sat down at their desks and got to work.

Seth, Anna, and Katy each had an index card in front of them. On each one their dad had written a Bible verse that he wanted them to memorize that week. Katy's verse was Proverbs 1:7. "The fear of the Lord is the beginning of knowledge," Katy read. "Fools despise wisdom and instruction." The verse was a familiar one and Katy pretty much had it memorized already, but she never could remember the reference. "Proverbs 1:7. Proverbs 1:7," she repeated to herself over and over. Katy saw Seth's card lying on his desk. It looked pretty long and Katy guessed it must have at least three verses written on it. Katy decided there were some nice things about being the youngest.

Math came after Bible. Mom handed each of her students a brand new math book. Seth's was the biggest and didn't have a single picture inside except for some graphs and charts. "Another nice thing about being the youngest," Katy thought. Her book had three yellow owls on the cover and the inside pages were full of brightly colored illustrations. The first lesson was easy. It was just a review of addition and subtraction and Katy flew through it. She looked at some of the lessons later on and got a little worried when she realized she had no clue how to do them. She hoped her mom would know how to explain it all to her.

The morning progressed smoothly. Katy liked it. She liked doing school at home. At 11:00 they had recess for half an hour. Lunchtime was at 12:30. Dad walked in the door just after the oven timer beeped letting them all know their pudgy pizzas were ready. Pudgy pizzas were one of Katy's favorites—two slices of buttered bread with pizza sauce and mozzarella cheese in the middle, grilled or baked to perfection.

After lunch, Seth, Anna, and Katy followed their dad to the den for history. Dad was a history buff and he had prepared a history lecture for their first day of school. Katy liked history fine, but her dad sounded as if he were talking to a room full of college students. Katy couldn't follow what he was saying, and found herself bored almost to tears. She had a blank piece of paper in front of her on which she was supposed to be taking notes, but she had no idea what to write. She wondered what Seth and Anna could possibly be writing down on their paper. Their dad finished by giving them an assignment of memorizing the presidents of the United States in order. They had until November 15 to have it done. He gave each of them a list of the presidents he had typed and copied so they could study them. Tears streamed down Katy's face as she looked at the long list of names.

"What's the matter, Katy?" her dad asked.

"I can't do this!" she said. "I can never memorize all those names." This was one of the harder things about being the youngest. She didn't understand why her assignment was the same as Seth and Anna's since she was so much younger.

"I'll help you," Anna volunteered.

Katy was wiping her eyes when her mom came back in the room after working on laundry. Mom asked her what was wrong.

"It's too hard," Katy said.

"Dad wouldn't give you an assignment unless he believed you could do it," Mom told her. She followed Dad into the hall as he prepared to go back to work. Katy could hear them talking.

"I'm sorry I got her upset," Dad said.

"She'll be okay," Mom answered. "Have a good afternoon." Katy saw her parents give each other a quick kiss and watched her dad head up the stairs.

When their mom came back in the room, she helped Anna and Seth get started on their science and then she took Katy out in the hall. As Katy listened to her mom talk about having a good attitude and being a hard worker, she tried not to cry. She wanted to whine and complain, but she decided not to. She didn't want to make the first day of school any worse. Mom sat down beside Katy at her desk and they worked on Katy's first science lesson together. Katy liked her mom being her teacher.

When it was 2:30, school was over. Katy didn't have a bit of homework besides memorizing the list of presidents. Since she had until November 15 to do that, she was in no hurry. She went outside to swing on the wooden swing in the crabapple tree in the front yard. When she saw her next door neighbor walking home from school, Katy ran to the sidewalk to talk to her.

"Hi, Chinway!" Katy called. Chinway and her family were from Nigeria. "How was school?"

"Oh, it was all right," Chinway answered. "How did you like homeschooling?"

"It was good," Katy answered. "Well, most of it. Want to play?"

"I better not," Chinway answered. "I should get started on my homework. See ya!" Chinway hurried on toward her house. List of presidents or not, Katy was glad that her parents had decided to homeschool. Her homework wasn't due until November! When

Katy's parents had first talked about homeschooling the summer before, Katy had been afraid it would make her too different. She didn't mind some differences, though, like being able to play outside while her friends worked on homework.

"But," Katy thought as she walked back toward her house, "I bet Chinway doesn't have to memorize all the presidents by November 15!" As Katy headed toward the back yard, she noticed the gate was open. She supposed Anna must be taking Sparky for a walk.

Katy ran to the playhouse in the back yard and climbed the rope ladder to see if she could spot Anna anywhere on the sidewalk nearby. After seeing no sign of her, Katy ran back around to the front and looked in the kitchen window. Her mom was standing at the sink.

"Hi, Mom!" Katy called. "May I walk around the block until I catch up with Anna and Sparky?"

"Anna's making cookies," her mom answered.

"She's not walking Sparky?" Katy asked.

"No, she's not," Anna answered, as she walked to the window and showed Katy her flour-covered hands.

"But the gate is open and Sparky's not in the back yard!" Katy was worried.

"What?" Anna cried. She hurriedly rinsed her hands at the sink and wiped them on her pants. She dashed out the side door of the house and ran to the back yard. "Sparky!" she called. "Sparky! Are you sure he's not back there?" she asked Katy.

"I didn't see him anywhere," Katy answered, running after Anna. Sparky was not there. Mom met the girls as they ran back to the front yard.

"You two go that way," Mom told them, pointing to the right. "I'll get Seth and he and I will go the other way. Sparky can't be very far away, Anna. Try not to worry. I'm sure we'll find him."

Katy and Anna ran to the end of the street together, then turned right. They called Sparky's name again and again, hoping all the time they would catch sight of him behind a bush or on the other side of a tree.

When they got to the end of the block, they turned right. Katy got excited for a moment when she saw a little black dog on the sidewalk several houses down, but she quickly realized the dog was on a leash and its owner was walking just a few yards behind it.

Anna and Katy continued to call Sparky's name. They soon passed the home of Mr. and Mrs. Robb, some of their favorite neighbors. Mr. Robb was working in his garden and heard them calling.

"Lost your dog?" he asked.

"Yes, sir," Anna answered. "Have you seen him?"

"Isn't he a real scruffy little fellow? Mostly black?" Mr. Robb asked.

"That's right!" Katy said, getting excited.

"I think he went that way," Mr. Robb told them, pointing the opposite direction from where they were headed. Anna thanked him and they turned to run the other way, calling Sparky's name all the time.

"God, please let us find him," Katy prayed. Just then she noticed something poking out from behind a tree on the other side of the street. She thought she saw it move, then she thought it was just a stick. Then she saw it move again. It wasn't a stick. It was Sparky's tail. "Sparky!" Katy called loudly. Sparky looked at her, then trotted off in the opposite direction.

Anna and Katy looked both ways and crossed the street. Anna wished she had thought to grab a dog treat before they left the house. She knelt down and called Sparky's name sweetly, but Sparky was more interested in sniffing the grass. Katy and Anna crept toward

Sparky slowly, one on each side of him. Finally Sparky discovered a piece of trash and became so interested in it that he didn't notice when Katy slipped her hand under his collar and grasped it tightly. When Sparky tried to walk away and felt a tug on his collar, he decided to roll over on his back and get a belly rub instead.

"Thanks, God," Katy whispered.

"Good job, Katy!" Anna said, relieved. "Thanks." Anna gave Sparky a kiss and Sparky licked her lips in return. Katy liked Sparky but she would never let him kiss her the way Anna did. Anna picked up her dog and they all three went home together. Anna put Sparky in the backyard. Sparky lay down in the grass and wagged his tail innocently.

After supper Katy went to her room to go over her memory verse one more time before bed. "Proverbs 1:7. Proverbs 1:7. Proverbs 1:7." Anna walked in before long.

"Want to work on the presidents?" Anna asked. Katy gave a slight groan.

"Not really," she said, "but I guess we could."

Anna had her list of the presidents in her hand. She climbed up to her bunk and sat down. "Repeat after me. George Washington."

"George Washington," Katy said. "That one's easy. I already know the first three. John Adams. Thomas Jefferson."

"Right. Next is James Madison," Anna told her.

"James Madison," Katy repeated. She lay down on her bunk and pressed her feet against Anna's mattress above her.

"No one who is helping her little sister memorize the presidents deserves to have her mattress pushed on from underneath!" Anna said, mostly teasing but slightly irritated.

"No one who rescues her sister's runaway dog deserves to be corrected on the very same day!" Katy replied.

"Well, anyone," Anna said, coming down the ladder, "who doesn't want to memorize the presidents deserves to be tickled unmercifully!" Anna leapt onto Katy's bed and began to do just that. Katy laughed until her stomach hurt and finally managed to blurt out, "Have mercy!" Anna did.

"Well, I have the first three down," Katy said. "That's enough for tonight. Besides, I have until November 15. Let's go in our closet playhouse and play Nertz." Nertz was a card game they often played and the closet playhouse in their room was one of their favorite places.

"You had the first three down before we started," Anna reminded her. "But I guess anyone who rescues her sister's runaway dog deserves to have her sister play cards with her." And Anna did.

3

Surprises

"Well, Katy," Mom said one Tuesday afternoon, "since tomorrow is your birthday I want you to decide what you would like to eat for each meal. Your birthday is going to be celebrated as a school-wide holiday!"

"That's pretty cool," Katy replied. "That didn't happen in school last year!" Homeschooling definitely had its perks. It didn't take Katy long to decide what she wanted to eat on her birthday. French toast for breakfast; pudgy pizzas, chips, and fruit salad for lunch; and sweet and sour chicken for supper.

"What kind of birthday dessert would you like?" Mom asked.

Katy thought about it, but couldn't decide. "Why

don't you surprise me," she finally said. Katy left her mom in the kitchen and wandered down the hall to her room. There was a sign on the door in Anna's handwriting that said *Please Knock!* Katy knocked.

"Come in unless you're Katy," came Anna's reply.

"Why can't I come in?" Katy asked.

"Don't you know better than to ask questions the day before your birthday?" Anna answered. Katy wandered back to the living room. She overheard her mom talking to her dad on the phone, giving him a list of things to pick up at the store on his way home.

"And why don't you pick up some chocolate chips," Mom finished, "because I think for dessert I'll make her a—" Katy covered her ears because she didn't want to spoil the surprise. Katy's mom came out of the kitchen and headed down to the basement.

"I need you to stay out of the basement for a little while," Mom said on her way down. "Secrets, secrets! You may go outside if you would like."

Katy felt a little lonely, but she knew she should feel glad that people were getting nice things ready for her birthday. She wandered outside and made her way to the playhouse at the back of the yard. Sparky lay in its shade.

Katy sat down beside him to rub his belly, but Sparky was tired of being still. He jumped up and ran to the other side of the yard, wagging his tail.

"Doesn't anybody want me around today?" Katy said out loud. She picked a blade of grass, held it between her thumbs, and blew, making a shrill whistling sound. Sparky perked up his ears and ran madly from one side of the yard to the other. Katy made another blow and Sparky ran again.

It was a warm day, warmer than usual for mid-September. Katy liked having a September birthday. The hottest days were past, but it wasn't too cold yet. The leaves were beginning to turn, but the world was still green and there were always flowers still blooming here and there.

Katy stood up, tucked in her shirt, and started practicing cartwheels in the middle of the yard. She had long wished she could take gymnastics, but her parents said it wasn't the best time for that. Katy figured the main reasons probably had to do with time and money, so she knew better than to pester them about it.

Katy imagined she was competing in the Olympic Games. She did a whole routine in the grass, complete with flips and cartwheels and different kinds of jumps and spins. Since she didn't have any music playing for her routine, she sang a song and tried to make her movements keep with the beat. She sang about flying through the sky like a shooting star.

When she was finished, she was completely out of breath. She imagined she was on the sidelines, waiting with her coach and her parents for the winners to be announced.

"Bronze goes to Yutong Chan of China," Katy said in a deep voice, pretending to be the announcer. "The silver medal goes to Heike Hennekemper of Germany. And the recipient of the gold medal is Katy Porter from the U.S.A.!" Katy turned around to her imaginary mom and quickly switched her voice to her own.

"I did it, Mom! I did it!" she said, jumping up and down. Just as she was about to step up onto the back porch to receive her imaginary medal, she heard Seth and Anna's voices mocking her in unison.

"I did it, Mom! I did it!" they said. The two of them burst out from their hiding spot beside the garage laughing. Katy felt her face turn red. She had no idea they had been spying on her.

Katy crossed her arms and put on a pouty face. "How long have you been spying on me?" she asked.

"Oh, we saw you flying through the sky like a star and everything," Seth answered.

"You're sneaky," Katy said. "That wasn't very nice."

"Oh, it was a good show!" said Anna, but Katy knew she was making fun of her.

"I'm telling Mom," Katy said.

"Wait, Katy," Anna said quickly. "We were just having fun with you."

"You were *making* fun of me," Katy insisted, her arms still crossed.

"Come on," Seth said, "let's play kickball." He knew Katy liked that game and he was hoping to keep her from going to tell on them. Katy knew exactly why he offered to play kickball with her.

"We were just playing," Seth added. He was starting to feel a little guilty.

"Come on, Katy," Anna tried. "Do you want to ride bikes?" At that moment Mom opened the back door. All three of them turned to look at her. Katy's arms were still crossed and she had a scowl on her face. Anna and Seth each put on a smile. Something was obviously up.

Mom asked what was wrong and Katy told her why she was upset. She said she didn't like it when people spied on her or made fun of what she was doing.

"That's understandable," Mom replied. "Seth and Anna, can you see how that would hurt her feelings?" Seth and Anna both said a bit reluctantly that they could, and they apologized.

"I just came out to ask for some help with supper," said Mom.

"I'll help!" Anna volunteered. She was anxious to make things right with her little sister, especially since tomorrow was her birthday. "That way you two can play kickball if you want." Mom turned and went back inside. As Anna started to follow their mom, she turned back to Katy.

"But really," she said, "you have to admit that you looked kind of funny twirling and jumping all over the back yard." Katy tried to keep from smiling, but it was no use. She bit her lips together, but the corners of her mouth gave her away.

"I guess I probably did," she admitted. The three of them laughed. Anna went inside and Seth ran to the shed to get a ball.

When Katy woke up the next morning, Anna was already out of bed. Katy got dressed and brushed through her long hair as quickly as she could. She skipped down the hall to the dining room. Anna was setting the table with placemats and cloth napkins. There was a bouquet of flowers from the yard in the center and at the far end was a stack of presents.

"Happy Birthday!" Anna said when she saw Katy.

"Well, here's the birthday girl," said Dad as he brought in a small pitcher of maple syrup. "How does it feel to be nine?"

"Oh, all right, I guess," Katy answered.

"Happy Birthday, Sweetie," Mom called from the kitchen. Seth came bounding up the basement steps, three at a time. He carried an oddly shaped package wrapped in scrap paper. The paper stuck out in strange places and Katy couldn't quite figure out how he had done it. It was Seth's trademark to wrap presents that way.

After their French toast breakfast, Katy opened her presents. Anna gave her a set of drawing pencils and a new sketchbook. Seth's strange package held a bag of marbles to add to her collection. Katy's parents gave her a jumprope, a beautiful bird figurine made of blue glass, and a new shirt and shorts set her mom made for her out of blue bandana fabric.

After Katy thanked them all, she expected her dad to rush off to work, but he lingered at the table with the rest of them.

"Aren't you supposed to be at work by now, Dad?" Katy finally asked. "Not that I'm trying to get rid of you, but do you realize what time it is?"

"Today is a holiday!" Dad replied. "I don't have to go to work on holidays."

"You mean you're taking the day off for my birthday?" Katy asked.

"That's right!" he said. Katy was delighted.

Mom didn't assign any math or spelling or science all day, and Dad didn't give a history lecture. Instead they all sat around the den and listened to Dad read the next two chapters of *Goodbye, Mr. Chips*, the book they were reading through as a family. While he read, Katy doodled in her new sketchbook and Seth played with Katy's new marbles. Anna sat on the floor with Sparky.

Later in the morning, Dad organized a game of Family Olympics in the back yard.

"I bet Katy will get first in gymnastics!" said Seth as they all headed out the back door. Katy gave him a look. "I'm serious! None of the rest of us can stretch and bend like you can!"

The Porters raced, threw balls into boxes, and competed to see who could jumprope and hula-hoop the longest. Katy won the hula-hoop contest when she kept it up for a solid eighteen minutes and thirty-two seconds. Seth won the shoe kick. No one expected his shoe to go all the way over the chain link fence and into Mr. Robb's garden, but it did! Mr. Robb was good-natured and didn't mind when the shoe landed on his squash plant. He just laughed and tossed the shoe back.

It was a good day. Katy enjoyed going to church that evening and getting to see her friends on her birthday. Her dad was the preacher for their church and he made an announcement during the devotional that it was her birthday. Mr. Battle pinched her cheek like he always did. Katy wondered if he would ever start thinking she was too big for that, but deep down she hoped he wouldn't.

"What did you do today?" Katy's friend Whitney asked her after class.

"Well, we had a Family Olympics in the back yard," Katy answered. "Dad stayed home from work and we didn't have to do school! It was fun. How was your day?"

"It was good!" Whitney answered. "We had a school assembly where we got to watch trained dogs do really cool tricks."

As they drove away from church, Katy felt a little sad. If she had been in public school, she could have seen the trained dogs on her birthday. She soon realized, though, that deep down she was glad that on her birthday she got to be at home with the people she loved the most. She was glad for Whitney that she got to see the dogs.

After they got home, Katy blew out nine candles on a chocolate chip brownie cake with fudge icing. Her mom had written *Happy Birthday Katy* in white icing across the top.

The next day life got back to normal with the Pledge of Allegiance and math assignments and a history lecture. Katy had enjoyed the break the day before, but she knew every day couldn't be like that. After history Mom gave them all a writing assignment. She wanted each of them to write a letter to the First Lady of the United States.

"Dad heard in a news story yesterday that the First Lady made some negative remarks about homeschooling," Mom explained. "I thought it would be a good idea for each of you to write her a letter and tell her what you like about homeschooling."

"I bet she'll get a lot of letters," Seth commented.

Anna agreed. "Homeschoolers really get into this kind of thing," she said. "You know, standing up for freedom and all that."

"Well, we should get into it," Mom answered. "In some countries, homeschooling is against the law."

"Do people in those countries do it anyway?" Anna asked.

"Some do," Mom said, "and some go to jail for it."

"Do you think the First Lady will write us back?" Katy asked.

"I don't know," Mom answered, "but hopefully she will at least read the letters."

Katy stared at the piece of notebook paper her mom handed her. She didn't know what to say. She finally picked up her pencil and began to write. She expected that she would have to write the letter over again after she was finished, but she surprised herself and her mom by doing a good job the first time. The only mistake she made was when she wrote that she was eight. She had to erase that word and change it to nine.

Dear Madam,

My name is Katy Porter and I am nine years old. My parents homeschool my brother and sister and me. I am glad they do. Since we homeschool, we get to be together every day. I love my family and I love spending time with them. I like being able to study the Bible during school. I like having my mom and my dad as my teachers.

I am glad that we are allowed to homeschool in America and I hope that never changes. If it does, there will be a lot of sad kids, including me.

God bless you.

Sincerely,
Katy Porter
Urbana, Illinois

4

A Contest

As the weeks went on, Katy began to notice how tired her mom looked. For Katy and her brother and sister, school went from 8:30 until 2:30, and then they were done. Katy didn't always notice the hours her mom sat at her desk making lesson plans and grading their papers and getting special projects ready. She started to pick up on conversations between her parents every now and then when her mom talked about how tired she was and her dad tried to encourage her. One day she overheard her dad say, "There has got to be an easier way to educate these children." She heard her mom crying after that. Katy hadn't meant to hear them, and she wished she hadn't. She went to Anna right away and told her what she had overheard.

"What do you think it means?" Katy asked.

"I don't know," Anna said. Even though she had been the most reluctant one to go along with the idea of homeschooling, Anna was comfortable with it now and didn't want things to change any more than Katy did.

"Maybe I'm not a very good student and mom doesn't want to be my teacher any more," Katy worried.

"I'm sure it's not that," Anna told her. "You've made 100% on all your math tests since school started!"

"I haven't been very good at history, though," Katy said. "And I stink at spelling."

"Don't worry," Anna reassured her sister. "Everything is going to be okay."

Anna left the room and Katy sat on her bed and thought. After a while she slid to the floor, pulled out her drawer under the bed, and took out her special box. She had hoped that homeschooling would give her some more keepsakes to put inside, but she hadn't added a single thing since school started. She opened it up and looked at the heart-shaped rock, the little doll, and the tangled necklace. She felt like adding something to her treasures, so she looked around her room. Her birthday cards were still displayed on the dresser beside the fish tank where her goldfish Wiggly Worm and Anna's fish Incognito were lazily swimming around. Katy picked up the card that said *For a Special Granddaughter*. Her mom's parents in Tennessee had mailed it to her with a check for fifteen dollars. Katy opened it and skimmed over the poem that was printed in the card. Then she looked at the words her grandparents had written by hand. Grandmother had written *You're real sweet. Have a big day.* Granddaddy had written *Happy Birthday, Stink Pot. You are someone worth living for.*

Katy had read the words when she opened the card on her birthday, but standing there in her room by herself, the words suddenly meant more than they had before. It was nice to be loved. Katy picked up the card from her parents and read what they had written. The words *Happy Birthday to our precious, beautiful daughter* were written in her mom's handwriting. Her dad had written *We love you, Katy.* The third card on her dresser was from her other grandparents and was signed *With love, Granddaddy Wes and Mema.* Katy decided to put all three of the cards in her box.

The next morning, Mom looked extra tired. Katy tried hard to do her best and keep a good attitude.

After Katy finished her math, Mom showed her an article in their homeschool group's newsletter about a fire prevention poster contest. It was open to all school kids in the area from first through fourth grade. Anna and Seth were too old for the contest, but Mom asked Katy if she would like to enter.

"I guess so," Katy answered. "What's the prize?"

"They are going to pick a grand prize winner from Urbana and a grand prize winner from Champaign," Mom explained. Champaign was the city right next to Urbana. The cities were so close together they were almost like one. "Each of the two winners will receive $100 for their school library. I'm not sure how that will work for homeschoolers, but I'm sure they can figure that out if they need to. Then they will pick one of the two grand prize posters to be made into a billboard somewhere in town."

"A billboard!" Katy exclaimed. "That would be so cool!"

"I'll call Dad and ask him to bring you some big white paper when he comes home for lunch," Mom told her. "So right now you can work on a design on some scrap paper, okay?"

"Sure!" Katy said. She was excited to have a special project all to herself. The article said each poster needed to have a slogan. The suggested slogan was "Test Your Detector, It's Sound Advice." Katy thought that most kids would probably just use that slogan since it was the one suggested, so she wanted to come up with her own. She thought she would have a better chance of winning if her slogan was original. One way or another, all the posters were supposed to encourage people to test the batteries in their smoke detectors.

Katy wrote down different slogans as they came into her head.

Are Your Smoke Detectors Doing Their Job?

Be A Detector Doctor

When Was the Last Time You Checked Yours?

Check Them Today. You'll Be Glad You Did.

Put Your Detectors to the Test

Katy looked over her list. She didn't think anything she had come up with so far was a winning slogan. She kept thinking and kept writing.

Are Your Detectors Detecting?
Go Home and Check. Check?
It's Alarming How Many People Don't Check Theirs
Let Their Sound Be Music to Your Ears

"This is hard!" she said out loud. Anna and Seth were busy with their schoolwork and didn't bother to respond. "Should I just use the slogan they suggested, Mom?" Katy asked.

"It's completely up to you, Honey," her mom replied. "This is your project."

Katy thought some more. She decided to start thinking about the picture she would draw instead of the slogan. How could she make a smoke detector look interesting? What would look good on a billboard? She thought her design should be simple so that people could see it from far away, just in case she won.

Katy imagined a smoke detector with arms and legs. She could draw a funny face in the middle. She looked up at the smoke detector on the ceiling of the den above where she was sitting. "I wonder if that one works," Katy thought. "Works," she whispered.

"I've got it!" Katy called out. "Listen to this. A picture

of a smoke detector with a face and arms and legs. It's holding a broom and a dustpan. The slogan is: *Make Sure Your Smoke Detectors Work!*"

"That sounds cute," Mom answered.

"Hmmm," Seth began. "It's a little cheesy, but I can see it on a billboard."

"That's pretty clever," Anna said. Katy liked it. She started sketching her design on scrap paper. She was anxious all morning for her dad to come home with the big paper.

When Dad arrived for lunch, he walked in the door with empty hands.

"Is the paper in the van?" Katy asked. "May I go get it?"

Dad slapped his hand against his forehead. "I knew I should have written myself a note for that. I'm sorry. I'll try to remember to bring it home tonight." Katy was quite disappointed, but there wasn't anything to do. The Porters only had one vehicle, and her dad would be taking it back to work after lunch. She would just have to wait.

Katy called her dad to remind him of the paper just before he left his office that afternoon. "I already have it," he told her. "I picked it up on my way back to the office after lunch."

Katy was elated. She worked on her poster after supper. She traced around a bowl from the kitchen to make a circle for the smoke detector. She drew it all in pencil first. She drew arms and legs coming out of the circle. She drew a dustpan in one hand and a broom in the other. Katy knew her handwriting wasn't the best, so she wrote the letters very slowly, trying to make them all the same size. She went over everything with crayon. Katy liked it. She could definitely imagine it as a billboard.

Just as Katy was finishing her poster, Anna walked in the den panting. "That dog!" she said as she flopped down on the couch.

"What's the matter?" Katy asked.

"He got out of the back yard again!" Anna told her. "I just had to chase him down the street. That's the third time this week! I don't get it. Dad just walked around the whole back yard and looked at the fence, but he didn't see any place Sparky could have crawled under."

"Maybe he jumps over it!" Katy suggested.

"Yeah, right," Anna said.

"Maybe he climbs it," Katy tried.

"I don't know," Anna said, "but this is getting old."

Mom took Dad to work the next day so she and Katy could have the van to deliver the poster. They took it to Mrs. Kerry, the leader of their homeschool group, who was going to turn in all the entries to the contest organizers the next day. The winners would be announced in two weeks.

The contest was on Katy's mind every day. She desperately wanted to win, but she tried not to hang her hopes on it. She knew her poster was just one of hundreds and hundreds of entries the judges would see.

On the day the winners were to be announced, the Porters' phone seemed to ring more than usual. Every time it rang, Katy felt her heart beat a little faster. Every time, though, she was disappointed. When it was time for bed, Mrs. Kerry had not called, so Katy gave up hoping.

Just as Katy was about to fall asleep, her dad walked into her room. "Katy?" he whispered. "Are you awake?"

"Sort of," Katy answered.

"You have a phone call," Dad said. Katy sat up on the edge of her bed. "I know it's late, but are you up to talking to Mrs. Kerry?"

"Mrs. Kerry?" Anna exclaimed from the top bunk. "Why is she calling so late?"

"Do you want to talk to her, Katy?" Dad asked again. Katy was groggy, but she cleared her throat and reached out her hand to take the phone from her dad.

"Hello," she croaked.

"Katy?" said Mrs. Kerry. "I am so sorry to be calling late, but I just couldn't wait until tomorrow. We've been out of town all day and we just got home. I had a message saying that one of our group's students received the grand prize in the Urbana poster contest. I called the person back and they gave me the details. It was you! You won, Katy!"

Katy's eyes widened and she leaped up off her bed. She twirled and danced around the bedroom as she listened to Mrs. Kerry tell her more details. Katy lay on her back on the floor and pedalled her legs in the air as if she was riding a bicycle upside down.

"Should we be worried, Dad?" Katy heard Anna whisper. "I think she's going crazy."

Katy smiled and shook her head as she mouthed, "I won!" Mrs. Kerry said that several posters, including Katy's, would be on display at Lincoln Square Mall beginning on Monday. Katy's heart was beating fast and she wasn't a bit sleepy anymore.

"So will mine be made into the bulletin board?" Katy asked.

"You mean the billboard?" Mrs. Kerry replied. Katy was embarrassed. Yes, that was what she meant. "Well, no, the judges chose the Champaign winner to be put on the billboard." Katy was disappointed, but she was too excited to stay that way for long. She was a winner. She was the grand prize winner for the whole city of Urbana.

When Mrs. Kerry was finished talking to Katy, she

wanted to talk to Dad again. Katy handed him the phone and he took it into the hall. Katy jumped up and down.

"I won! I won!" she cried. "I really, really won!"

"What did she say about the billboard?" Anna asked.

"The Champaign winner gets to be on that," Katy told her. "But it's okay. I don't mind . . . too much."

When he was off the phone, Dad came back into the bedroom. "Congratulations, Katy!" he said, putting his arm around her shoulders. "Mom will be so excited when she gets home."

"When will she be home from Mrs. Conner's house?" Katy asked. Shirley Conner was a family friend. She often called Katy's mom and needed to talk for a long time. Katy's mom tried to be a good friend because she knew Shirley needed one. Shirley had a hard life. Shirley was especially down that day, and had asked Mom to come over after supper.

"I don't know when she'll be back," Dad answered, "but it might be a while. You better go on back to bed."

"Will you please not tell her that I won?" Katy begged. "I want to tell her myself. If I fall asleep before she gets home I can tell her in the morning. Please?"

Dad agreed to keep it a secret. "Oh," he said, "Mrs.

Kerry said that since you don't exactly have an official school library, the contest organizers are going to give the prize money to the Urbana public library. You get to choose the books they purchase with the money." Katy began to think about what books she would choose.

When Mom heard the news the next morning, she was almost as excited as Katy. That very day the children's librarian at the Urbana library called Katy to ask what books she would like them to purchase with her prize money. Katy told the lady about a series of historical fiction she liked, which the library didn't have. The librarian said she would order the books as soon as she could.

"Now, let me make sure I have your name spelled correctly," the librarian said. "Is it K-a-t-i-e P-o-r-t-e-r?"

"My first name is spelled K-a-t-y," Katy told her.

"I'm glad I asked!" the librarian said. "We're going to put a bookplate in the front of each of these books that says 'Donated by Katy Porter.' I'll make sure we spell your name right."

"Thank you!" Katy said. She couldn't wait to see her name in all those books.

The following Monday after Dad got off work, he

picked up the rest of the family and they all went to Lincoln Square Mall together. They found the posters near one of the entrances. Katy's poster and about twenty others were on display. All the posters had ribbons, but only two had a big purple ribbon that said *Grand Prize*. One was on the Champaign winner's poster, and the other was on Katy's. Katy beamed when she saw it. Her

mom told her to stand beside the poster and smile so she could take a picture. Katy knew exactly where the grand prize ribbon would go once the poster display was over.

"That ribbon," Katy thought, giving it one last look before they left the mall, "will fit perfectly in my box."

5

Being Different

Seth had the presidents memorized by the end of October. He said them for Dad without making a single mistake. Anna almost had them down herself, but Katy was still struggling to keep everyone straight between Abraham Lincoln and Calvin Coolidge. Their November 15 deadline was getting pretty close. Katy tried to work on them every day, but some days she forgot. She had a big note beside the fish tank on her dresser reminding her to practice, but she didn't always notice it.

One Thursday night the Porter family went to their favorite pizza restaurant for dinner. Every Thursday night was the Porters' family night. They usually ate a special meal at home, but this night Dad had suggested they go out. This didn't happen very often and Katy was excited. As they headed out the door, Katy grabbed a baseball cap and put it on. She wasn't going to be out in the sun, but she just felt like wearing it.

As the Porters sat around the table looking at their menus, their server named Samantha came to take their drink orders. Dad told her they would all take water. Samantha pointed out that kids under ten get free drinks and asked, "What does he want?" Katy was surprised she thought Seth was under ten, but when she looked up she saw that Samantha was looking directly at her. Katy felt her cheeks turn hot as she realized that Samantha thought she was a boy. She quickly whipped her ponytail around to the front and Samantha seemed embarrassed.

"May I have lemonade?" Katy asked her mom.

"Sure, Honey," Mom replied. Samantha nodded and mumbled an, "I'm sorry," as she headed to the kitchen.

"She must have bad eyes. You do not look like a boy," Anna assured her sister as soon as the waitress was out of earshot.

"Absolutely not," Mom added.

"Then why would she say that?" Katy asked, quite hurt.

"She just wasn't paying attention," Seth told her.

"She was probably thinking about the fight she had with her boyfriend yesterday," Anna said.

"Anna," Mom said reprovingly.

"Well, whatever she was thinking, she obviously wasn't paying attention," Anna said.

"You're beautiful," Mom told Katy. "But, you shouldn't be wearing that baseball cap at the table. I didn't really notice you were even wearing it."

Katy took the cap off her head and laid it on the seat beside her. She reached back and pulled the ponytail holder out of her hair. She wanted to let her long hair fall around her shoulders so it would be more obvious she was a girl.

Samantha soon came out of the kitchen with a tray of four waters and one lemonade. Katy realized that hurt feelings or not, getting a free lemonade was one of the nice things about being the youngest. As Samantha walked toward their table, she tripped on the leg of a nearby chair. Despite her efforts to steady the tray, all of the glasses slid to the floor in a wet and icy mess. Samantha's eyes immediately filled with tears. She left the mess and rushed back to the kitchen.

"Great service tonight," Seth commented sarcastically. In a few minutes, two other employees came out of the kitchen. The young man started to clean up the mess on the floor. The lady carried another tray with five waters and walked to the Porter's table.

"Hi, I'm Jeanne," the lady said. "I'll be taking care of you tonight. I'm sorry about the mess and about your long wait."

"Is Samantha okay?" Mom asked.

"She's . . . well," Jeanne hesitated then finally said, "her husband left her yesterday and she's just about to fall apart. I probably shouldn't have told you that. Don't mention it, please. Everyone had water, right?" Jeanne said, placing a glass at everyone's place.

"Well, actually, she ordered lemonade," Dad said, pointing to Katy.

"Oh, I'm sorry," Jeanne said. "Samantha forgot to tell me. I'll be right back." Jeanne went back to the kitchen and soon returned with Katy's lemonade.

Dad gave Jeanne their pizza order and Jeanne assured them it would be right out. As she started to leave their table, Jeanne looked at Anna and Katy. "You girls sure have beautiful hair," she commented.

Anna and Katy looked at each other and smiled. Katy wondered if Samantha had told Jeanne about her mistake thinking Katy was a boy, or if Jeanne just thought of making that comment out of the blue. Either way, it did make Katy feel a little better.

The pizza and breadsticks were as good as ever. After they finished, Dad put his arm around Mom and seemed to get more serious.

"Kids," he said. Seth, Anna, and Katy could tell by the way he talked that something was up. They wondered what was coming. "I want you to know that your mother is the most wonderful woman in the whole wide world."

Mom smiled. "You're sweet," she said.

"I hope you realize the sacrifices she is making to homeschool you," Dad continued. "It takes a lot of work."

"But I wouldn't trade it for anything," Mom added quickly. "I really love spending all day with the three of you."

"Thanks, Mom," Seth said. Anna and Katy added their thanks as well.

"I really do appreciate it," Anna added. Then she asked, "Are you trying to tell us something? Have we done something wrong?"

"Oh, no," Dad assured her. "I just wanted to make sure you realize how blessed you are. Well, I guess since the pizza is gone we should head home." Dad paid the bill and they all headed out to their brown minivan.

"My hat!" Katy exclaimed. "I left it on the seat. May I go back and get it?" Dad gave her permission.

When Katy went inside the restaurant, Jeanne was cleaning the Porters' dirty dishes off their table.

"Excuse me," Katy said. Jeanne didn't hear her, so Katy said it again a little louder. "Excuse me." Jeanne turned to her and smiled. "I left my hat," Katy told her. Jeanne had not noticed the hat, so it still lay where Katy left it on the seat. Jeanne stepped aside so Katy could reach it.

"I can tell you have a special family," Jeanne said. "Do you homeschool?"

"Yes, we do," Katy answered, mystified that Jeanne had guessed. Jeanne could tell Katy was surprised.

"I can just tell sometimes," Jeanne told her. "You've got you a good family, girl. Don't ever forget it."

"I won't," Katy said. "Thank you." She turned and hurried out the door. Dad had pulled the van up beside the restaurant. Katy climbed in.

"Our waitress just said she could tell that we homeschool!" Katy suddenly felt glad in a new way that God had put her in this family.

When the Porters turned onto their street, Anna saw Sparky on the corner.

"Dad, stop!" she yelled from the back. "Sparky's out again!" Dad stopped the van and Anna opened the side door. She called Sparky and this time instead of running the other way he ran straight for the van, jumped inside, and leaped on the back seat beside Anna. "Good boy, Sparky," Anna said. Seth closed the door and Dad drove on to their house.

"What do you mean by 'good boy'?" Seth asked. "He seems like a pretty naughty boy to me."

"Well, he came when I called," Anna said defensively. "That was being a good boy."

"Yes, but he was being good after being bad," Seth said. "You're sending him mixed messages. How is he supposed to learn the difference between good and evil?"

"Oh, Seth," Anna replied, getting a little annoyed at her brother. "He's a dog. You sound like a psychologist."

"I'll send you a bill," said Seth, "and one for the little

dog, too." Katy saw her parents smile at each other in the front.

While Anna returned Sparky to the back yard, Mrs. Conner called. She said her day had been really hard and asked Mom if she would come over as soon as she could. Mom said she would come, but told her that since it was their family night she would need to wait until after the kids went to bed.

The Porters all gathered in the den downstairs to listen to Dad read the last three chapters of *Goodbye, Mr. Chips*. After a quick game of Nertz, which Anna won, it was time to get ready for bed. As they cleaned up the cards, Mom told them all goodnight, kissed Dad, and headed to Mrs. Conner's house.

Katy woke up when she heard the garage door open a few hours later and knew her mom must be home. Since she was awake, Katy decided to go say hello. She headed down the hall and heard her parents talking in the kitchen.

"I am exhausted," her mom was saying, "but I can't go to bed yet because I don't have tomorrow's lesson plans laid out."

"There has got to be an easier way to educate these children," Dad replied. They were the same words Katy had heard him say before. Katy knew she wasn't supposed to be hearing this conversation, so she hurried back to her bedroom. As she tiptoed down the hall, she heard her mom start to cry.

"I'm trying to help, Eva," Dad said, frustrated. "We went out to eat tonight so you wouldn't have to cook."

"I appreciate it, Jack, but I just don't think—" Katy was back in her room now and couldn't hear any more. She didn't like it when her parents' voices got so intense.

Anna heard Katy crawl back onto the bottom bunk. "You okay, Katy?" she asked sleepily. Katy didn't answer. "What's the matter?" Anna asked, more awake now.

"Mom and Dad are talking in the kitchen," Katy told

her. "It sounds like they are about to have an argument. Mom is crying. She has too much to do and Dad said there has to be an easier way to educate us."

Anna and Katy didn't know what else to say. They both lay silently on their beds, wondering what changes might be coming. Finally they both fell back to sleep.

The next day, Anna and Katy tried hard to be helpful. They cleaned up the kitchen after breakfast and lunch without being asked and were extra cheerful when they did their schoolwork. Their half-hour recess time turned into an hour because Shirley Conner called their mom and needed to talk again. Katy didn't mind the extra long break a bit, but she noticed that her mom seemed stressed when they finally got back to school because they were off schedule.

Katy played outside with Chinway and Chinway's younger brother that afternoon. They played tag, but it wasn't much fun with just three people, so pretty soon they just sat down in the grass.

"So what's it like homeschooling?" Chinway asked. "What do you do all day?"

"Oh, it's kinda like regular school," Katy answered. "We do history and science and math and all that. We have recess and break for lunch." Chinway asked Katy if she still liked it.

"I do," Katy said, "but my mom is getting pretty worn out from it all, and it's only October. I'm starting to wonder if things are about to change for my family again."

"How?" Chinway asked.

"I'm not exactly sure," Katy said with a lump in her throat, "but I overheard my parents talking and they sounded pretty stressed out."

Chinway and her brother soon had to go inside to do their homework. Katy decided she should go home and study the presidents. She found her mom in the kitchen. Katy went up to her and threw her arms around her waist.

"I love you, Mom," she said. "Thanks for homeschooling me."

"You're welcome, Honey," Mom answered. She put down the spoon she was using to stir the soup on the stove and gave Katy a big hug back.

"If we ever go back to public school," Katy asked, "do you think people will still think we are a nice family? You know, like the waitress did last night?"

"Before we decided to homeschool you were afraid it would make you too different," Mom answered. "Now it sounds like you're afraid going back to public school will make you too different!"

"I like being homeschooled," Katy answered. "I like being different. I don't want anything to change."

"I don't know what will happen in the future," Mom said, her arms still wrapped around Katy. "No one does. But we can be a nice family if you kids go to public school or if you go to a private school or if we homeschool. The school isn't the most important thing. It's what's inside our hearts that matters. Our family can be different from the world no matter what kind of school you go to."

"But I thought you decided to homeschool because you thought it was best," Katy said.

"We did," Mom answered. "We decided to homeschool because we felt that was the best decision for our family. But that doesn't mean we are the best. I want you to remember something, Katy. Being in public school doesn't automatically make one kid better or worse than any other kids. Homeschooling doesn't either. It's always what's inside that counts."

Katy nodded. She wanted to ask if they had figured

out an easier way to educate Seth and Anna and herself, but she decided not to. "I guess I better go see if I can get it straight whether Woodrow Wilson came before or after William McKinley."

"That's my girl," Mom said. "You can do it!" Katy wasn't so sure, but she headed to her room to study just the same.

6

On Stage

The following Monday, Katy woke up excited. She popped out of bed and climbed up the ladder to Anna's bunk.

"Anna, wake up!" Katy said in a loud whisper. "We have to get ready. Don't you remember?"

"Remember what?" Anna asked in a sleepy voice.

"We're going to see the musical today! We have to be ready by 7:30!" Katy climbed back down the ladder and hurried to feed the fish and get dressed.

Before they started homeschooling, the Porters had to get ready this early every day, but they were out of practice. It was 7:49 when they pulled out of the driveway to take Dad to work and head to the big theater across town. Mom had arranged the field trip and she wanted to get there first to pick up the tickets. She was afraid the other eight families would be waiting for them, but they weren't.

"Homeschoolers are supposed to be late!" Anna said with a smile. The other families soon arrived, followed by several busses full of school children.

Katy loved to see live performances, and she was quite excited. She had been in two short skits at church and decided that she loved acting. She wished she could be in a play at a real theater. Her ears always perked up when she heard about a production happening somewhere. She wondered what it would be like to audition, but she had never been allowed to participate. She understood her parents' reasonings about busy schedules and ungodly influences, but she still dreamed of having a lead role in a grand production someday.

The homeschool group arrived at the theater first, so they got to sit on the front two rows. While she waited for the musical to begin, Katy flipped through the program over and over. She liked the way the title of the musical, "Jazzy Four," was written across the front to look like music notes. Mom had told them the production was going to be about a singing group that traveled around to different places during the 1920s. Katy looked at the cast list and saw that the members of the Jazzy Four were the only actors in the show. She had been expecting a large cast and wondered if just four guys could really put on a good musical.

As soon as the performance began, Katy realized that the whole audience was a part of the show. The four actors talked to them as if they were all living back in the 1920s and were really at this performance. Katy loved it. She loved the songs and the choreography. There was a piano on stage and one of the actors played song after song as the four of them sang and made jokes and talked about their interesting lives on the road as they traveled across the country.

Partway through the production, the pianist asked the audience if anyone knew how to play the song "Heart and Soul" as a duet on the piano. Mom had taught Katy how to play that song last summer. Katy timidly raised her hand. Several other kids and adults in the audience put a hand up, too.

"Who likes to play the top part?" Roger the pianist asked. Most of the hands stayed up. Then he asked, "And who likes to play the bottom part?" Katy enjoyed playing both parts, so she kept her hand up for both questions, raising it a little higher each time.

Before Katy knew what was happening, the pianist walked down off the stage and took her by the hand. Katy looked at her mom, who just smiled back and seemed as curious as Katy as to what was about to happen. Roger led Katy back up the steps onto the stage. Katy was surprised by how bright the lights were. She squinted and could hardly see the hundreds of faces that were staring at her.

"So you're a pianist, are you?" Roger asked. Katy nodded as she felt her face turn red. "Don't be shy," Katy told herself. "You're on stage! This is your chance!" She tried to shake away the nervous feeling that had come over her and make the most of being on a real stage.

"Well, have a seat here by me," Roger said, leading Katy to the piano bench. Katy sat down beside him and tried to remember to sit up straight. Her eyes slowly adjusted to the lights. Her lips and her throat suddenly felt very dry. She found herself smiling and not able to stop. This was fun.

"Oh, I almost forgot to ask," Roger said. "What is our young pianist's name?"

"You mean me?" Katy answered.

"Well, I don't see any other strangers on the stage," Roger teased back. Katy felt her cheeks get a little hotter. "Or anyone else who is young, for that matter, besides myself." The other three actors pretended to be offended by Roger's joke.

"I'm Katy," Katy answered.

"Well, Katy," Roger instructed, "show your stuff. Twice through on 'Heart and Soul.' And a-one, and a-two, and a-you know what to do!"

Katy's hands shook as she put her fingers on the piano keys and began to play. She made a mistake the first time through, but she picked back up and the second time she played it perfectly.

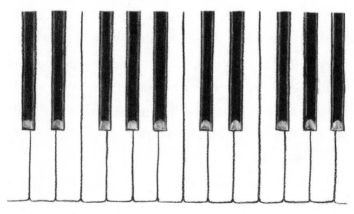

"Let's give it up for Katy, folks!" Roger called out when they had reached the end of the song. The whole theater applauded. Katy smiled so big that her cheeks started to hurt, but she couldn't stop. Roger took her by the hand again and led her to the center of the stage. Music started playing through the speakers and the four actors linked arms and began kicking their legs back and forth to the beat. Roger and Mike linked arms with Katy. Katy joined right in with the dance. The audience clapped again. When the music was over, Roger went to the piano and picked up a piece of paper that was lying on top. He pulled a pen out of his pocket and quickly wrote something on the paper.

"Wasn't she wonderful, ladies and gentlemen?" Roger asked the audience, getting them started in another round of applause. "To honor your fine performance, we would like to present you with this certificate declaring you an honorary member of the Jazzy Four." Roger handed Katy the piece of paper and Katy thanked him. Roger whispered that she could go back to her seat now.

Katy walked back down the steps and sat down between her mom and Anna. Her eyes had to readjust to the darkness. Mom put her arm around Katy's shoulders and Anna squeezed her leg. They both whispered, "Good job!" at the same time. Seth gave her a thumbs up.

Katy looked down at the certificate in her lap. Since she was on the first row, the lights were bright enough that she could read it. It said:

HAVING PROVEN JAZZY WORTHINESS,

WE HEREBY PRONOUNCE

Katie

TO BE AN

HONORARY MEMBER OF THE JAZZY FOUR

At the bottom of the certificate were four blanks where each of the actors had signed his name before the show began. Of course Katy wished that Roger had spelled her name correctly, but she didn't let that bother her. She knew right where the certificate would go after she showed it to her dad that evening.

During dinner Dad enjoyed hearing Katy tell all the details of her theatrical debut. Katy enjoyed hearing her mom and Anna and Seth tell what it was like from the audience while she was on stage.

"When you dropped me off at work this morning," Dad said when they were all done, "I thought you were just going to *watch* this musical. I didn't know you were going to be playing a piano and dancing with a bunch of strange men!"

"Dad!" Anna cried. "You're making it sound like she's a saloon girl or something."

"I'm just teasing," Dad told her. "I wish I could have seen it."

After the kitchen was cleaned up, Katy took her certificate to her room and showed it to Sugar Plum, Wiggly Worm, and Incognito. She opened her drawer under the bunk bed and lifted out her box. The purple ribbon from the poster contest was the last thing she had put inside. Katy laid her Jazzy Four certificate on top. Just then, Anna burst into the room.

"Katy, look!" she cried, showing her a big brown envelope. "I just got the mail. We got a letter from the White House!"

"Really?" Katy asked as she looked closely at the envelope in Anna's hand. "First Class Do Not Bend," she read aloud. "But it doesn't say we can't open it!"

"We shouldn't open it without Seth because it's

addressed to him, too," Anna said. "Come on downstairs. I think everyone else is in the den."

Anna and Katy hurried to the basement. "Look, everybody!" Anna called. "We got a letter from the White House!"

They all gathered around and stared at the envelope together. The return address said, "The White House, 1600 Pennsylvania Avenue NW, Washington, DC 20500." It was addressed to Seth, Anna, and Katy Porter.

"She even spelled my name right," Katy noticed excitedly.

Dad pulled out his pocket knife. "Shall I do the honors?" he asked. He carefully slipped his knife under the flap of the big brown envelope and slid it across the edge, being careful not to tear it. Inside was a piece of cardboard to keep the letters from being damaged in the mail. There were three separate letters. Dad handed one to Seth, one to Anna, and one to Katy.

Katy gently traced her finger around the gold circle at the top of the stationery. Inside the circle was a gold embossed eagle that looked like the eagle on the back of a quarter. Under the circle were the words, "The White House, Washington," in blue. The letter read:

Dear Miss Katy Porter,

Thank you for your recent letter. I did not mean to offend anyone in the comments I made recently regarding education. It sounds like your parents are training you well and I commend them for that. I know that the job of being a teacher is not an easy one.

No matter where you receive your schooling, I hope you will study hard and stay in school until you graduate. This will help you to become a responsible citizen of this great country.

May God bless you, and may God continue to bless our Nation.

Katy looked closely at the signature at the bottom. Seth said he thought it was just a stamp, but Katy thought it looked real. Either way, she could hardly believe she was holding a letter from the President's wife in her very own hands.

"Keep those somewhere safe," Dad told them.

"May I put mine in my special box?" Katy asked. Dad told her she could, as long as she made sure that it did not get bent. Mom gave Katy an empty folder so she could be sure the letter stayed flat. Katy hurried upstairs and put the letter on top of the Jazzy Four certificate in her box.

"Two things in one day, Wiggly Worm!" Katy said to her fish. "Not bad!"

Katy suddenly thought of the conversation she had accidentally overheard between her parents. "God," she prayed, "please let us keep homeschooling. I really, really want to."

Katy realized that if she wanted to keep homeschooling she needed to make sure she did her part. She picked up her list of presidents from the dresser and covered over part of the list with her hand. As she practiced, she slid her hand down after she said each name to make sure she was right. "Theodore Roosevelt, William Howard Taft, Woodrow Wilson, Warren G. Harding, Calvin Coolidge . . . ."

7

Thankful

On the morning of November 15, Katy asked Anna to help her go over the presidents one more time. Today was the deadline. Anna and Katy had to recite them for their dad during history time after lunch, whether they knew them or not. Katy was sure Anna could do it, but she wasn't quite as confident about herself. She still had a tendency to mix up Harrison, Cleveland, and McKinley.

When it was time, Anna went first. She and Dad went out of the den while Seth and Katy waited. Seth lay on the couch with his eyes closed. The pressure was gone for him since he had already completed the assignment. While Katy waited for her turn she reviewed the presidents of the late 1800s over and over in her head.

Anna came back in the den with a smile on her face. "I did it!" she said. "Your turn, Katy!" Katy moaned as she turned and left the den. Her dad stood at the bottom of the stairs.

"Ready?" he asked with a big grin on his face.

"Maybe," Katy answered. Then she began, "George Washington, John Adams, Thomas Jefferson, James Madison . . . ." Only once did Katy start to say the wrong name. Her dad made a grunting sound and Katy immediately realized her mistake and corrected herself. When she got to the end Dad put up his hand for a high five.

"That's my girl!" he said. "See? I knew you could do it. You've got a good head on those shoulders and it's got some good brains inside."

Katy smiled. She was relieved that it was all over, relieved that she had done as well as she had, and quite proud of herself. When her dad first gave her the assignment over two months ago, she really didn't think she could do it. But she had.

After Dad had finished history class for the day and gone back to work, Mom said it was time to be finishing their costume projects for the upcoming Thanksgiving program the homeschool group was doing. Each family had been invited to put together a skit or a song or a special project and share it with everyone else the Thursday before Thanksgiving. Katy was going to dress as a Native American and Seth and Anna were dressing as Pilgrims. They had chosen a song about thankfulness to sing together.

The only thing Seth lacked for his costume was a hat. He and Mom went to the sewing machine to finish it together. Anna sat on the couch sewing lace on her blouse by hand. Mom had helped her make a grey wool skirt to go with it. They hadn't yet figured out how they were going to make the jacket to complete her costume.

Katy sat on the floor with a tray full of beads in front of her. One by one she carefully chose beads and strung them on a cord to make a necklace. When it was finished, she started on a bracelet to match.

They were all engrossed with their costume making and didn't notice that it was past time for school to be over. Katy didn't mind. A project like making a Native American costume didn't really feel like school anyway. It was 3:28 when the doorbell rang. Mom went upstairs to answer it. Katy followed, curious about who might be on their front porch. It was Chinway.

"Sparky's out again!" Chinway blurted out as soon as Mom opened the door. "And this time I saw him do it! You won't believe it, but he opened that gate himself and just trotted right on out! He stood on his hind legs and put one paw on the fence and then with the other paw he just opened the latch as easy as pie!"

"Are you serious?" Mom asked.

Katy was still standing on the top step. She turned around and called down to the den, "Anna, Sparky's out again!" Anna ran up the stairs two at a time.

"Do you know which way he went?" she asked.

"He went that way," Chinway told her, pointing left. Anna hurried out the door.

"And she knows how he's getting out!" Katy called after her. Anna didn't stop, so Katy added quietly, "But I guess you're more interested in getting him back first."

Anna soon returned to the yard with Sparky in her arms. Chinway was waiting with Katy in the front yard. She told Anna what she had seen and Anna was amazed at what an intelligent dog she had.

"He might be smart," Katy said, "but he's rather naughty!" Anna took Sparky to the back yard and asked Katy and Chinway to make sure he didn't get out while she went to find something to secure the latches. She walked to the shed at the back of the yard and came out with a broken leash and a rusty padlock. The clip still worked fine on the leash, so she clipped it in the gate latch on one side of the house and hooked the padlock in the gate on the other side. The rusty padlock didn't lock anymore, but it would keep Sparky from being able to open the gate.

"There," Anna said, walking back to Katy and Chinway. "That should do it. This explains why I kept finding the gate open. It never occurred to me that Sparky was the one opening it! Thanks, Chinway."

"No problem," Chinway told her. "I want to be a detective when I grow up. See ya later! I'm helping my mom make cookies for the fall festival at school." Anna and Katy watched Chinway run back to her house.

"I remember the fall festival last year," Katy said. "I guess there were some good things about public school."

"Of course there were," Anna said. "Public school wasn't all bad, just like homeschooling isn't all good."

"And homeschooled kids aren't all good just like public school kids aren't all bad," Katy added. "It's all a mixture."

"I do miss seeing my friends every day," Anna said, "but I'm glad I get to see more of you and Seth. You guys are good friends."

"You, too," Katy told her.

Seth and Mom finished his hat that evening. Anna and Katy still had more to do on their costumes, so they worked on them on Saturday. Katy's costume was made of a synthetic leather material they found on clearance at the fabric store. Mom had helped her make a simple dress and Katy sat on the floor making three-inch slits all the way around the bottom to create a fringe. Next she cut a triangle out of a leftover piece and cut fringe around it to make a shawl.

"Are you still planning to make a jacket?" Katy asked.

"If we can figure out an easy way to do it," Anna answered, still sewing the lace on her blouse.

The next day at church, there was a visitor in Katy's class. Their teacher, Mrs. Lanford, introduced the girl as a friend of hers named Beth. Katy could tell by the way Beth was dressed that her family probably didn't have much money. Beth's hair was in a ponytail, but it was messy and looked as if she had slept with it up like that. She wore a fancy black and white dress, but it was too small for her and the grungy tennis shoes on her feet didn't match the dress at all. Beth didn't answer any of the questions Mrs. Lanford asked and Katy wondered if she had ever heard the story of Joseph and his coat of many colors.

Katy sat next to Beth as they all worked on their Joseph worksheets. "How old are you, Beth?" she asked, trying to be friendly.

"Nine," Beth answered quietly without looking up.

"I am, too!" Katy said. "I just turned nine in September. Do you have any brothers or sisters?"

Beth nodded. "I have a little brother named Jackson. He's six. He's here, too."

"Maybe I can meet him after class," Katy said. Beth just nodded and didn't look up.

After class Mrs. Lanford asked Katy if she would like

to sit with them during the assembly. Katy usually sat with her own family on Sunday mornings, but she didn't think her mom or dad would mind this exception. She was right. Katy's parents knew that Mrs. Lanford just wanted Beth to have a friend.

Before the worship time started, Jackson peppered Mrs. Lanford with one question after another about what he had learned in his class.

"Did that guy really make the blind man see?" he wanted to know.

"Who? Jesus?" Mrs. Lanford asked. "He certainly did! Jesus is the Son of God who worked miracles."

"I ain't never heard of nobody doing nothing like that," Jackson said. "I think it's all made up."

"Nobody tells lies in church," Beth told him.

"But they said that Jesus made people see just by talking to them!" Jackson said.

"He did," Mrs. Lanford told him.

"Just like that?" Jackson questioned.

"Just like that," said Mrs. Lanford. Jackson still looked skeptical as the song leader stepped up on the stage to begin the first song. Beth sat down quietly next to Katy. Mrs. Lanford whispered to Jackson and told him to sit down, too, but he didn't. The song leader told everyone to turn to number 716 in their songbooks.

"What's a songbook?" Jackson asked out loud. Mrs. Lanford put her finger to her lips. She pulled a songbook out of the pocket on the back of the seat in front of her and handed it to Jackson. "What number we supposed to sing?" Jackson asked in a loud voice. Mrs. Lanford put her finger to her lips again and quietly turned to number 716.

All during the assembly, Jackson went back and forth from his seat to the floor, and once he started to crawl under the row in front of them. Mrs. Lanford grabbed his foot and pulled him back out. He dropped his songbook on purpose again and again. He was full of questions about what was happening and what it all meant.

When six men walked to the front to serve the Lord's Supper to the congregation, Jackson looked at Katy and asked what they were doing.

"They're serving the Lord's Supper," Katy whispered back. "Shhh."

"What's the Lord's Supper?" Jackson asked in a loud voice.

"It's something we do to remember Jesus," Katy whispered.

Mrs. Lanford whispered to her visitors that only the people who had decided to live for Jesus would take a bite of the bread and drink from the little cups of juice.

"I want some!" Jackson said out loud. Mrs. Lanford shook her head and Jackson crossed his arms and pouted.

When the men went to the front again to pass out the collection plates, Jackson commented, "They're doing it again! I hope the kids get to do it this time." When the collection plate came down their row he asked Katy what it was for.

"People put in money to pay for church things," Katy answered in a whisper.

All through Dad's sermon, Jackson continued to fidget and whisper. He asked questions about what Dad was saying, he asked why the chairs were teal, and he asked what was in the maintenance closet on the other side of the auditorium.

"This is boring," Jackson finally said near the end of the sermon.

As the congregation sang a song together after

the sermon was over, Katy looked up at her dad, who still stood in front of the congregation. He looked uncomfortable as over and over he tried to adjust his suit coat. At first Katy thought he was just nervous. Then she wondered if maybe he was annoyed at all the disturbances that had come from her row during his sermon. She then noticed that something seemed to be wrong with his coat. Both sleeves were several inches too short. She wondered how the coat could have shrunk.

When the assembly was finally over, Jackson and Beth said they were hungry.

"What did you have for breakfast this morning?" Mrs. Lanford asked them.

"We didn't have no breakfast," Jackson answered. "That's why we're hungry."

Katy was shocked. She knew that kids in Kenya and Guatemala and places like that had to go without breakfast, but she hadn't thought about kids right here in Urbana not having enough to eat. Mrs. Battle had been sitting behind them all through the assembly and overheard Jackson's answer. She offered to take the children to the kitchen and get them a snack. Mrs. Lanford said that would be wonderful. At the mention of food, Beth's eyes lit up and Jackson's smile spread across his face from ear to ear.

"I know it seems surprising that they would act like that," Mrs. Lanford told Katy after they were gone, "but I don't think they have ever been to church before. It was all new to them. They have a tough time at their house."

On their way home, Katy told her family about the adventures on her row.

"I could tell you were having quite a time of it," Dad said. "I had a hard time keeping my focus while I was preaching."

"I'm sure you did," Mom said. "I was feeling sorry for you."

"Is that why you kept pulling at your sleeves?" Anna asked.

"I saw you doing that, too, Dad," Katy said. "What was wrong?"

"I don't know what it was," Dad answered. "This suit coat just doesn't feel right today. I've worn it plenty of times before."

Mom leaned forward to look over at Dad in the driver's seat and get a better look at the coat. "Jack!" she exclaimed. "No wonder the sleeves are too short! You're wearing my coat! It goes with that skirt Shirley Conner gave me." Seth, Anna, and Katy all burst out laughing. Dad did not think it was quite as funny as everyone else did. He shook his head.

"That's what I get for being in a hurry on a Sunday morning," he said. "I think it's safe to say that's the first time I have ever preached while wearing my wife's clothes."

"I took the outfit because Shirley wanted to give it to me," Mom said, "but I didn't think I was likely to ever wear it. I never dreamed *you* would!" They all laughed again, even Dad.

When they got home, Dad anxiously pulled off the suit coat. "I'm finished borrowing this, Dear, if you want it back."

Mom took the coat and turned it around to look it over more carefully. "You know, Anna," she said, "I think this coat could become part of your costume for Thursday."

"Suits me," Anna said. "Pun intended. *Suits* me. Get it?"

"Well, just as long as it never *suits* me again, you can do whatever you want with it!" Dad answered.

On Thursday morning, Seth, Anna, and Katy put on their costumes and practiced their song one more time. The coat turned out to be just what Anna's outfit needed. Mom had helped her alter it so that it went with her costume perfectly.

Dad took time off from work to come to the program and hear his kids sing. They all listened to the other songs that were performed and watched the skits. Mrs. Kerry's daughter Tonya recited a Thanksgiving poem.

Katy's stomach was full of butterflies when it was their turn to sing. She clutched her shawl so tightly that her knuckles turned white, but everything went fine and no one's voice cracked and the audience clapped when the song was over.

Everyone enjoyed a Thanksgiving potluck after the program. The tables were covered with food. Katy sat beside Tonya to eat. They had seen each other at several homeschool group events and were becoming friends.

As Katy ate a piece of chocolate pie, she thought about Beth. She wondered if Beth had ever enjoyed a meal like this. She hoped Mrs. Lanford would bring Beth to church again so they could become friends, too.

8

Happiness

All of the Porters looked forward to Christmas break. Their first semester of homeschooling was almost over, and they were all ready to take some time off. Katy wondered if their last day of school before their break was going to be their last day of homeschooling, period. She kept thinking about hearing her dad tell her mom there had to be an easier way to educate their children. She wondered if they had figured out what that easier way was going to be.

On their first day of Christmas break, Katy and her mom were alone in the basement and Katy decided to come right out and ask.

"Mom," she said, "have you figured out an easier way to educate us?"

Mom was mystified as to what Katy meant. "What are you talking about?" she asked.

"Well," Katy said, "I didn't mean to, but two different times I overheard Dad tell you there has to be an easier way to educate us. I know you're tired and stressed. I just wondered it you had figured anything out."

Mom smiled. "Something about school has to change in January, but we haven't figured out what yet. I did get pretty worn out this past semester."

"I'm sorry we wore you out," Katy answered.

"Oh, Sweetie, it's not your fault. You are all great students. It's just a lot of work to get lesson plans ready and grade papers and things. I'm just tired."

"I hope we keep homeschooling, Mom," Katy said.

"I hope so, too," Mom answered. "We're going to see what we can do."

Katy went upstairs. She sat on the couch in the living room and stared at the Christmas tree they had all decorated together two weeks before. Katy looked up when Dad walked through the living room on his way to the basement, but he didn't look at her. He was obviously upset. Katy wondered why. She heard the den door slam downstairs and then heard her parents' voices rising.

Soon Mom came up the stairs crying and headed down the hall. Dad soon followed, looking even more upset than he had before. Katy heard their bedroom door close—hard.

"Why do they have to do this?" Katy wondered. Anna came into the living room and asked Katy if she knew what was going on. Katy shook her head. Before long Seth came upstairs. It was lunchtime, but their parents were still in their bedroom. The three of them just waited.

Their mom finally came out of the bedroom and went silently to the kitchen. Katy and Anna followed her. Mom was crying as she heated up some leftover potato soup.

"Do you need any help?" Anna asked. Mom said they could set the table. They all worked in silence. Dad joined them a few minutes later, looking cross. Seth came into the kitchen, too.

"Let's just pray in here and then get our soup," Dad said. He asked Seth to pray. It felt like a heavy weight was on everyone's shoulders. After Seth thanked God for their food, Katy decided to try to help lift it off.

"I don't want to eat until I see everyone smile," she

said cheerfully. She turned to her dad and said, "You first!"

"I guess you won't be eating then," Dad said. He turned and left the kitchen and huffed down the hall.

Katy was crushed. Her lip began to quiver and she couldn't hold back the tears. She ran to the couch downstairs in the den and buried her head in a pillow.

After a little while, Dad came in. "I'm sorry, Katy," he said. "I was wrong." Katy turned to look at her dad. She swallowed hard. Katy usually had a really hard time with the words she knew she was supposed to say. Did she forgive him? How could she forgive him when she still felt crushed? Then she remembered hearing once that forgiveness doesn't mean forgetting, but it's a decision to let go and move on.

"I forgive you," she said. Dad stroked Katy's hair and gave her a hug. "What's the matter?" she asked.

"It's not worth talking about," he said. "I wasn't very nice to your mom and I'm sorry."

"Are you guys going to be okay?" Katy asked. Dad nodded. Mom soon came in the den.

"Do you two want some lunch?" she asked them. "Katy, your party at the Lanfords' house starts in an

hour. You'd better come eat something before you go."
Katy had completely forgotten about the Christmas
party Mrs. Lanford was hosting that afternoon for the
kids in her class at church.

"Are you guys okay?" Katy asked her mom. She
wanted to be sure of the answer before she did anything
else.

"Yes, Sweetie," Mom told her. "I'm sorry we had
an argument, but we've worked it out now. See?" Katy
watched her parents give each other a kiss. "We're still in
love," Mom said with a smile.

Katy knew they were, but she was getting tired of the
tension that had steadily been building in their family.
She was ready for things to feel lighter and more at ease.
She had a feeling that once the decision was made about
school, things would get better. Her dad had been right
when he said they couldn't keep going on like this.

After lunch, Dad drove Katy across town and walked
with her up the steps to the Lanford's front door. The
Lanfords lived in an older part of town. Their street was
paved with bricks and big trees lined both sidewalks.
The Lanfords' house was like a setting in a book. It
had beautiful wooden floors and was full of interesting

souvenirs they had brought back from their travels around the world. A wicker basket seat hung from the ceiling in the living room. Katy hoped she would be able to have a turn to sit in it.

Dad rang the doorbell. Katy took her dad's hand and looked up at his face. He smiled down at her.

"It's nice to see you smile," she said.

Dad squeezed her hand and said, "I'm sorry about earlier."

"I forgive you, Dad." Katy told him. It was easier to say it that time.

Mr. Lanford soon opened the door. "Come in, Katy, come in!" he said warmly. He had a special way of making people feel important. "We're glad you're here." Dad told Katy he would pick her up in a couple of hours and headed back to the van.

"The children are all playing downstairs while Mrs. Lanford finishes up the snacks in the kitchen," Mr. Lanford told her. "Just follow me." Katy followed him down the stairs to the basement. Two of the boys were playing ping-pong and some of the girls were playing with Chinese jumpropes. Katy was glad to see that Beth was there.

"I didn't know you were going to be here," Katy said to her, "but I hoped you would be."

"Mrs. Lanford wanted me to come," Beth answered. She looked uncomfortable as she stood off to the side. Katy picked up a Chinese jumprope and asked Whitney to join them so they would have a threesome. Beth jumped, but she still didn't smile very much.

Mrs. Lanford soon brought down plates piled with cookies and fruit. She put them on the ping-pong table, so the boys' game had to stop. Mr. Lanford carried in a big punch bowl filled with a fruity drink. Everyone found a place to sit, some on the steps, some on stools, and some on the floor.

When the snacks were almost gone, they all sang Christmas carols together. Then they gathered around the ping-pong table for the craft Mrs. Lanford had prepared. The Lanfords had recently been to the beach and brought back a bucket of shells. Mrs. Lanford told each of the children they could choose one to keep. Katy chose an oval-shaped shell that was blueish-purple on the outside and pearly white on the inside. Mrs. Lanford set containers of glue and small plates of beads and sequins around on the table and told everyone to decorate their shells. When they were finished, Mr. Lanford used a special tool to punch a small hole in each shell so they could be strung with thread to hang on a Christmas tree.

Katy and Beth were the last ones to leave the Christmas party. After everyone else had been picked up, they and Mrs. Lanford waited upstairs in the living room for Katy's dad to arrive. Mr. Lanford walked in and saw the basket chair hanging empty because Katy

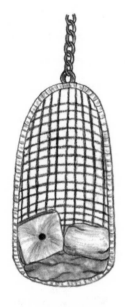

and Beth were both too shy to ask if they could sit in it.

"Katy, don't you want to have a seat in the basket chair?" he asked.

"Beth can have a turn," Katy answered. Beth eyed the basket chair and smiled. She had been wanting to sit in it ever since she arrived. She walked across the living room and had a seat. She swung gently back and forth. Katy could tell she liked it. Part of Katy wanted to be sitting in the chair herself, but most of her was glad she was letting Beth have a turn.

Dad arrived soon. Beth let Katy have a quick turn in the chair before she left. Katy thanked the Lanfords and walked back down the brick pathway with her dad to the brown minivan. She told him about the party and showed him her shell ornament. When they got home, Katy hung the shell on the Christmas tree beside her little porcelain mouse ornament, which was one of her favorites.

The next day in Bible class, Mrs. Lanford invited everyone to have their parents bring them to the nursing home on Tuesday evening so they could all sing Christmas carols together. She told everyone their siblings could come, too.

When Katy told her family about it, they decided that they would all participate. On Tuesday evening they bundled up and piled in their van. When they walked into the nursing home, the smell made Katy's stomach churn.

"Why does it smell so bad?" Katy asked her mom.

"Not everyone here is able to keep themselves clean anymore," Mom whispered. "We just need to smile and love them anyway." Katy raised her shoulders and tried to bury her mouth and nose in her coat to hide the smell, but her mom tapped her arm in a way that said, "Don't do that, Katy." Katy reluctantly lowered her shoulders back down.

A man in a wheelchair sat just inside the front door. He leaned forward slightly and stared ahead with a blank expression. A thin stream of drool hung from his mouth. "Merry Christmas," Mom said to him with a smile. He didn't reply, but looked right at Katy.

"Merry Christmas!" she managed to say. Katy thought she saw a faint smile on his face.

The Porters joined the Lanfords in the activity room and they all waited a few minutes for more people to arrive. Whitney and her mom came, as well as two other families. Mrs. Lanford passed out a song sheet to everyone and they walked together out of the activity room into the first hall. Most of the residents were in their rooms, but some were wandering up and down the hall. Many of them brightened up when they heard "Joy to the World" and "Hark, the Herald Angels Sing." Some of the residents even sang along with them.

One lady motioned for Katy to come over to her. Katy went, even though she didn't really want to. "I like your singing!" the lady said brightly.

"Thank you," Katy answered.

"You're a pretty little girl," the lady said. "What's your name?"

"Katy," she answered. "What's yours?"

"Aimee," the lady replied. "I'm from New York. I bet Santa Claus is going to bring a nice girl like you all sorts of fun things." Katy just smiled.

"What are you going to do for Christmas?" Katy asked her.

"My daughter will come see me," Aimee answered. "This place isn't too bad, but I sure wish I could be at home."

Katy thought about how sad it must be to spend Christmas in a nursing home. She wished there didn't have to be so many sad people. She thought about Samantha at the pizza restaurant, and she thought about Beth and Jackson. She almost felt guilty that her own life was full of so much happiness.

As they left the nursing home, Katy had a lonely feeling—not for herself, but for Aimee. She wanted to do something about it, but she didn't know what.

When the Porters got home, Dad called for a family meeting in the den downstairs.

"Well, the first semester of Porter Academy has come to a close," Dad began. "I think you three have a pretty amazing teacher. Let's give her a hand." They all clapped and Mom smiled. "While the first semester was a success," Dad continued, "it was just too much for your mom. She is worn out. Something has to change."

"Are we still going to homeschool?" Katy asked.

"Yes," Mom answered, "but it's going to be different. Your dad and I have realized that we haven't been homeschooling the way we should. We have been putting too much focus on academics and not enough focus on things that matter for eternity, like serving people and making a difference in the world. When we started homeschooling, I thought I needed to recreate public school with a bulletin board and the Pledge of Allegiance every day. But we don't need to do things exactly like public schools do. We need to do things that are right for each of you and right for our family.

"We have realized that the most important thing for our family is for the three of you to learn to live for Jesus. Jesus isn't as concerned about math tests and science quizzes as He is about taking care of the elderly and helping people who are in need.

"Now, we're not throwing all the books out the window. Academic learning is important and we expect you all to learn what you need to know to graduate. But, academics are not the only way we need to be preparing you for life. I feel like school has been a ton of bricks we've been trying to carry around. We want our family to have a lifestyle of learning that really matters."

"Are we still going to have to do things like memorize all the presidents?" Katy asked.

"Yes," Dad said with a smile. "You still need to know math and history and science because that's learning about the world God made and knowing about His world will make you a better person. But we want to spend more time focusing on what is eternal—what is really going to matter in the end."

"I'm excited," Mom said. "I think doing school like this is going to be a lot more fun."

Katy hadn't heard her mom sound so happy about school in a long time. Katy was excited, too. Things already felt lighter.

9

Christmas

Katy felt like a cloud had lifted from over their family. After the meeting in the den, everyone seemed more cheerful. Katy looked forward to the new kind of school that would begin after Christmas.

All of the Porters were busy on Christmas Eve. In keeping with their family tradition, they had all secretly prepared for the talent show that would happen in the evening. Also in keeping with their family tradition, most of them had waited until the last minute to get ready.

Katy had been working hard to memorize the passage in Luke chapter 2 about angels visiting the shepherds after Jesus was born. The year before she had recited the first part of the chapter when Jesus was born and laid in a manger. This year she was adding the part about the shepherds. She planned to add the wise men next year. She knew that memorizing verses for school was a good thing to do and she didn't mind it, but she enjoyed this secret memory work even more.

Katy and Anna were also working on a skit to perform for the rest of their family. Katy was going to be their dad and Anna was going to play the part of their mom. They had been talking for weeks about what they could include in their skit, but it wasn't until the afternoon of Christmas Eve that they went to their room and decided they should practice at least once before the talent show.

Throughout the day, the various members of the Porter family were also busy secretly wrapping the gifts they were going to give each other on Christmas morning. Katy had used some of her own money to buy a roll of snowman wrapping paper she used for the four gifts she was giving.

In the late afternoon, Katy and Anna joined their mom in the kitchen to prepare their Christmas Eve feast. Katy cut the cathedral window cookies while Anna arranged the German chocolates in a fancy dish that was shaped like a Christmas tree. They always looked forward to the delicious variety of cheese and crackers, fruit, nuts, chocolates, cookies, and candies they had every Christmas Eve. Their mom had made her annual batch of cheeseball to top it all off. They laid everything out on the red and green table runner on a card table set up in the den. Katy loved the familiar feeling of getting everything ready as though important guests were coming over, when really it was just going to be the five of them like it always was. She enjoyed giving and receiving gifts on Christmas morning, but she enjoyed Christmas Eve even more.

When the food was ready, they all gathered in the den for the talent show. Anna went first and sang a beautiful song about the birth of Christ. On Seth's turn he took everyone to the computer and showed them a program he had made where you could decorate a Christmas tree with different kinds of lights and ornaments. After everyone had a turn to add something, Seth pressed a key that made the tree light up and "Jingle Bells" played.

Katy went next and recited the verses she had memorized from Luke chapter 2. Her voice quavered a little bit. She didn't understand why she was nervous around just her family, but she was. Nervous or not, she made it through without missing a word.

Dad and Mom went next and performed a comedy routine they had learned soon after they got married. Seth, Anna, and Katy rolled with laughter.

Anna and Katy's skit was last. They pretended it was a busy Sunday morning and rushed around the room quoting phrases their parents often said and doing things they often did. Mom laughed so hard she cried. Dad chuckled all the way through the skit and let out three of his good strong belly laughs, which Katy always loved to hear.

"That was good," Dad said when they were finished. "Cruel, but good!"

"We're just trying to be true to life," Anna said with a smile.

"You pay closer attention than I thought!" said Mom.

"Well, have we worked up enough of an appetite for the feast?" Everyone agreed they had. They piled their Christmas plates with goodies from the table and got settled onto the couch and chairs for the annual viewing of the movie *It's a Wonderful Life*. They only watched this movie on Christmas Eve, but they watched it every Christmas Eve. Katy loved seeing George Bailey and Uncle Billy and Zuzu at the same time every year. It was like seeing old friends.

When the movie was over and the food was cleaned up, Katy brushed her teeth and climbed into bed on the bottom bunk. When her dad came in to say goodnight, Katy asked him why he always cried at the end of *It's a Wonderful Life*. Dad smiled and gave an embarrassed sort of laugh.

"It's a good movie," he said. Katy thought it was a good movie, too, but her dad seemed to like it in a different and deeper way. She supposed that was because she was nine and he was an adult.

On Christmas morning, Katy woke up first. She jumped out of bed and climbed up to Anna's bunk.

"Merry Christmas, Anna," she whispered. Anna stirred. "Merry Christmas!" Katy said again. Anna woke up and stretched. After a moment she looked around and saw Katy smiling at her from the ladder.

"Hi," Anna said. "Merry Christmas. Want to come up?" Katy climbed the rest of the way up the ladder and snuggled under Anna's quilt with her.

"Why does Dad cry every year at the end of *It's a Wonderful Life*?" Katy asked.

"He identifies with George," Anna told her. "You know, other people go off and do big things and get rich and famous, but here's George working away in a little town. George has a lot of friends and he's making a big difference, but it's not the sort of difference a lot of people take the time to notice or say anything about."

"How is that like Dad?" Katy asked.

"Well, being a preacher hasn't exactly made Dad rich and famous," Anna replied, "but he's making a difference in a lot of people's lives. And at the end of the movie when Harry Bailey says that George is the richest man in town, I bet maybe Dad feels like he's saying that to him and it makes him feel good."

"How do you figure out things like that?" Katy asked.

"I pay attention," Anna said. Katy supposed it had something to do with Anna being eleven instead of nine.

After they lay in bed a few more minutes, Katy heard footsteps in the hall that sounded like her dad's. She headed down the ladder and decided to follow him to the kitchen. When she got to the kitchen, he was already getting out the ingredients for cinnamon rolls.

"Merry Christmas, Dad," Katy said, giving him a hug. He hugged her back and kissed the top of her head.

"Merry Christmas, Sweetie."

"May I help you?" Katy asked.

"Sure!" he told her. "You can mix up the icing."

Katy got the powdered sugar out of the cabinet and the milk out of the fridge. She made a mess pouring the powdered sugar in a bowl. She poured in a little milk, trying to be careful not to get too much. She had made the icing before and knew it was easy to get too much milk. She added a little more at a time until the icing was the perfect consistency without any lumps.

After Dad made the dough and rolled it out in a rectangle, Katy helped him spread butter all over it and sprinkle it with cinnamon and sugar. Dad rolled it up and Katy got to help with her favorite part: slicing the roll to make the cinnamon rolls. They laid them on a pan and put them in the oven to bake. Katy thought about asking her dad if he felt like George Bailey sometimes, but she decided not to. It seemed like it might spoil something if she did.

After breakfast, the Porters opened their gifts. Katy liked the way her family exchanged gifts with everyone taking turns and everyone else watching instead of everyone ripping into them at the same time.

Since Katy was the youngest, she handed out the gifts she was giving first. Anna liked the striped slipper socks Katy had picked out for her and Seth was glad to have three new plastic baseballs to hit in the back yard. Katy gave her mom a little wooden rooster she had found at a craft fair back in the spring and had kept hidden under her bed all these months. Dad liked the new deck of cards, even though he said Katy would probably beat him if he played anything with her.

The gift exchange lasted the whole morning. Katy was glad it turned out better than the year before when their dad gave their mom a bread machine. Mom had tried to be nice and polite, but everyone could tell she wasn't excited about the gift. Dad thought she would be, but she had never even wanted a bread machine. Katy remembered Seth asking Anna what the big deal was.

"You're not supposed to give a lady an appliance as a gift, Seth," Anna had told him. "You'd better remember that when you're married." Katy was surprised that Seth didn't already know that. She knew it, and she was four years younger. She supposed it was one of those things guys just had a hard time understanding. This year Dad gave their mom earrings, a sweater, and a beautiful ceramic serving bowl. After all of the presents were open, Katy noticed Anna giving their dad a thumbs up when their mom wasn't looking.

For lunch they ate their annual Christmas dinner of pizza. Dad had begun this tradition when Katy was very small. He said he didn't want Mom wearing herself out cooking on Christmas, so they would just have pizza instead. For supper there were plenty of leftovers from their Christmas Eve feast to do it all over again.

The day after Christmas the Porters left for a week in Tennessee, where Dad and Mom had both grown up. Katy enjoyed seeing her grandparents, great-grandparents, aunts, uncles, and cousins. Mama Sue served them chess pie and peanut butter fudge like always and Granddaddy took them to the diner to sit on the spinning stools and eat ice cream. Grandmother gave Katy a shirt she had made her for Christmas. Everyone made Katy feel special as they always did. Katy wondered if anyone was making Beth or Aimee feel special.

When the Porters got back to Illinois, there were only a few days left before the new semester began. Katy looked forward to school starting almost as much as she had looked forward to Christmas break.

10

Back to School

As Katy sat in her usual spot completing her math page for the day, she wondered if the new way of doing school was really going to be much different. The first day back had begun pretty much the same as the days before Christmas break, except that they didn't say the Pledge of Allegiance.

"So does this mean we're just not going to be as patriotic anymore?" Seth had asked, trying to be difficult.

"Of course not, Seth," their mom had replied. "It just means we're not going to do public school at home anymore. We're going to homeschool."

After lunch, Mom told the kids about a special project they were going to begin. It sounded like a lot of fun to Katy. She guessed that this was one of the things her mom had meant when she said they were going to focus more on things that were eternal.

The elderly people at their church had a group called the Golden Agers. Every month the Golden Agers did something special together. Sometimes they went on a day trip and sometimes they gathered at the church building for a special program. Mom told Seth, Anna, and Katy that next month, the three of them were going to be the special program.

"Are you serious?" Anna asked, rather shocked. "What are we supposed to do?"

"We could sing our thanksgiving song!" Katy suggested.

"In February?" Anna said. Katy realized her idea wasn't very good.

"I thought maybe you could do a puppet show," Mom said.

Katy was excited. It wouldn't be quite the same as being in a play, but it would be kind of close. Seth didn't really care one way or the other what they did, but Anna was not excited about it.

"I really don't like to get up in front of people," she said.

"If we do a puppet show, you can stay behind the curtain!" Katy told her.

"Just think how much the Golden Agers will enjoy it," Mom said. "It will mean so much to them."

"Come on, Anna," Katy encouraged, "you're really good at writing scripts and things. Just think about all those plays we've done down here with Jenny and Rachel!" Katy and Anna had performed many plays for their parents in the basement with their friends Jenny and Rachel from church. Anna was often the mastermind behind the scripts.

"I guess it might not be so bad," Anna said with a sigh, "as long as I get to stay behind the curtain."

The phone rang and Mom answered it. "Oh, hi, Shirley," she said. "Hold on just a minute." Mom put the phone down and gave instructions to Seth, Anna, and Katy. "It's Shirley Conner," she told them, "so I don't know how long I'll be. I want you to work on choosing a Bible passage to be the basis for the puppet show. I'll be back as soon as I can." Mom headed out of the den and up the stairs so she could wash dishes while she talked— mostly listened—to her friend.

"Hmmm," Seth wondered aloud. "How about when

all those kings are in subjection to Kedorlaomer and there's a big battle and Lot gets kidnapped!"

"Seth," Anna said, "must you always be so obscure?"

"Hey, it's in the Bible!" Seth replied. "I read it this morning. It's in Genesis 14."

"I know it's in the Bible," Anna told him, "but I'm just not sure it would make the best puppet show."

"It would be exciting!" Seth said. "Old men like war movies."

"You're supposed to say 'elderly.'" Katy reminded him. "Besides, we're doing a puppet show, not a movie."

"He's just trying to be difficult," Anna told her. "He knows we aren't going to do a puppet show about Kedorla— whatever his name is."

"How about a puppet show of when Jesus was born?" Katy suggested.

"Well," Anna said, trying to be diplomatic, "I'm sure that would make a great puppet show, but it probably would have been better to do it in December instead of February. Not that there's anything wrong with talking about the nativity all year, but people don't usually expect a program about it in February."

Katy knew Anna was right, but it was the first story

that popped into her head when she tried to think of one, probably because their Christmas decorations were still up and she had just been looking at the little wooden nativity scene on the bookshelf across the room.

"Let's try to think of something not too typical, but not too obscure," Anna suggested. They tossed around different ideas, some from the Old Testament and some from the New Testament. They started exploring ideas that weren't exactly stories, such as the Beatitudes in Matthew or the Armor of God in Ephesians.

"I've got it!" Seth said. "How about that part in Ecclesiastes that says, 'There is a time for everything.' You know, there is a time to plant and a time to dance and all that."

"That sounds great!" Anna said. "That could be really fun."

"Not too typical, but not too obscure," Katy observed. "Perfect."

Anna grabbed a notebook and they started brainstorming about how they could make puppets act out the different verses. By the time their mom finished her conversation with Mrs. Conner and rejoined them in the den, they only had one verse left to figure out.

"How can we act out, 'There is a time to kill' without one puppet having to kill another one?" Anna asked.

"Mom!" Katy burst out. "There's a huge spider right behind you!" Everyone looked to see an enormous, slightly fuzzy spider on the wall behind their mom. Mom took off her shoe and gave the spider a decided *whack*. It shriveled up and fell to the floor.

"That's it!" Anna cried. "One of the puppets can whack a bug! That shows the perfect time to kill!" Everyone laughed. They all thought Anna's idea was brilliant.

The following Sunday, Katy sat beside Beth as they waited for Mrs. Lanford to begin their class. Beth wore a new pair of brown shoes with tiny embroidered butterflies on the toes.

"I like your shoes," Katy told her.

"Thanks!" Beth replied. "Mrs. Lanford gave them to me for Christmas."

"All right, boys and girls," Mrs. Lanford said, getting everyone's attention. "Let's start by playing Draw Your Sword." Everyone knew how to play the game except Beth. Mrs. Lanford suggested that Beth be her helper this time since she had never played the game. Katy knew it wasn't only because Beth hadn't played the game before that Mrs. Lanford made this suggestion. Since Beth hadn't been coming to church very long, Mrs. Lanford didn't want her to be embarrassed when she couldn't keep up with the other kids who had been going to church since they were babies. Mrs. Lanford was good at thinking of things like that.

Beth moved over to sit beside Mrs. Lanford while Katy and the other kids stood up around the table. Katy picked up her Bible and put it on her shoulder, just as all the other kids did. Mrs. Lanford told Beth when to say, "Draw your sword!" to begin each round.

"Why do I say that?" Beth wanted to know.

"Because the Bible is like a sword for the Christian," Mrs. Lanford told her. "We can use what it teaches us to fight off the devil so we can keep following Jesus."

As soon as Beth said, "Draw your sword!" all the kids put their Bibles on the table. Mrs. Lanford then read a Bible reference and the first one who could find it and start reading it in their own Bible won that round. Mrs. Lanford told Beth to keep score.

The first reference Mrs. Lanford gave was Luke 6:31. Katy knew where to flip in her Bible, but she was so anxious to get there first that her fingers trembled slightly and she had trouble turning the pages. Whitney found the verse first.

"Treat others the same way you want them to treat you!" Whitney quickly read. Beth made a mark by Whitney's name on the score sheet. Katy closed her Bible and put it back up on her shoulder, and all the other kids did the same.

"Draw your sword!" Beth called out. Katy quickly placed her Bible on the table.

"Psalm 91:2!" Mrs. Lanford said. Katy knew that Psalms was near the middle of the Bible. She opened her Bible and somehow it opened right to the very page she was looking for. She quickly read the verse out loud.

"How did you find it so fast?" her friend Megan wanted to know.

Katy shrugged. "I just opened right to it!" she said with a smile.

The game continued until Katy and the others had searched for ten verses. Whitney won the game by finding four of the verses faster than anyone else.

Toward the end of class, there was a knock on the door. Mrs. Lanford opened it and Mr. Wade walked in.

"Pardon the interruption, Mrs. Lanford," he said. "I just have a quick announcement for the kids." Mr. Wade went on to tell them that he was working on writing a script for an Easter play. All the kids at church were invited to be in the cast if they wanted to be. They would start practicing in February and practice every Sunday night until they performed the play the Friday before Easter.

Katy could hardly believe it. She was beside herself with excitement. She was sure her parents would let her be in this play! "A real play," Katy said to herself. "A real play! I'm going to be in a real play!" Katy wondered what kind of part she would get.

"What's the play going to be about?" Beth asked. "Is it going to have the Easter Bunny in it?"

Katy and some of the other kids laughed. They all knew that the play would tell the story of when Jesus died on a cross and came back to life and not have anything to do with the Easter Bunny, but Beth didn't. She didn't know that Easter was about anything more than bunnies and egg hunts. Katy immediately felt bad for having laughed when she saw how embarrassed Beth looked.

Mr. Wade explained what the play would be about and said he hoped everyone would participate. He told them he would announce it to the whole congregation during the worship assembly and tell their parents how they could sign up their kids to be in it.

As soon as class was over, Katy chatted with Whitney, Megan, and Beth. Everyone was excited about the play, but Katy felt like she must be the most excited of all. She had dreamed of being in a play for so long.

Katy's parents said yes, she could participate. Anna wanted to be in it, too. Seth would have enjoyed being in the play, but it was only for kids up through sixth grade, so he was too old.

That night the Porters went back to the church building for the evening assembly. Katy and Anna joined the other kids in the fellowship hall for their Sunday night class, taught by an older lady named Dorris Large. As she headed down the hall, Katy repeated the memory verse for that week. If she could say it without any mistakes, she would earn another star sticker. Every time one of the kids earned five star stickers, they got to pick a prize. Katy had four stars on her chart already and she was sure she could get another one that night.

Before class began, Katy went up to Mrs. Large to say her verse. She said it perfectly, earned her fifth star sticker, and looked forward to the end of class when Mrs. Large would let her have her prize.

Mrs. Large often used puppets in her class. Katy and Anna looked at each other when Mrs. Large stepped behind the puppet stage and began her puppet skit for that night. They were both thinking about the puppet show they would do behind that very puppet stage for the Golden Agers in just a few weeks. Katy was sure Mrs. Large would be in the audience when she and Seth and Anna performed "There is a Time." It made her a little nervous to think about doing a show in front of such a puppet expert.

Katy sat between Anna and Megan as they all watched the puppet skit about being honest. At the end of class, Mrs. Large called Katy to the front. She was the only one who had earned a prize that night. Mrs. Large held up her small metal mailbox that was filled with candy and small toys.

"Close your eyes, Katy!" Mrs. Large told her. "Reach in and pull something out." Katy closed her eyes and reached her hand into the mailbox. She felt pieces of candy and pencils and a tiny car, but she didn't want any of those. She felt something square and slightly soft, but couldn't figure out what it was. She thought about just pulling it out, but she didn't want to be disappointed with her prize. Katy opened her eyes a tiny bit, just enough so she could see into the mailbox and see what was in her hand, but not enough so that anyone else could see that her eyes were open. The square object was an orange pencil topper with the Statue of Liberty on it. Katy closed her eyes tightly again and decided the pencil topper would be fun to use while she did her schoolwork. She pulled it out of the mailbox and opened her eyes.

"Thank you!" she remembered to say. Katy sat back down between Anna and Megan. Mrs. Large said a prayer to end the class. Katy clutched the Statue of Liberty pencil topper in her hand. She had a horrible feeling in her stomach. She had cheated. Mrs. Large had told her not to look, and she had. Katy felt terrible, but she didn't know what to do. She couldn't bring herself to go back up to Mrs. Large and tell her what she had done, especially after having watched a puppet skit about being honest.

Katy hurried out of the room. She wove through the crowded hall looking for her mom. She found her in the foyer talking to Megan's mom. Katy tapped her mom's side and Mom held up a finger to tell her to wait. Tears began to stream down Katy's cheeks. She was miserable. Her hand was sweaty from clutching the pencil topper so tightly. She wished she could fix things by just throwing it away, but she knew that wouldn't take care of it. Besides, then she wouldn't have a prize.

As soon as her mom realized that Katy was crying, she broke off her conversation with Megan's mom. "Katy, what's the matter?" Mom asked.

Katy didn't want to say it out loud, especially not in front of Megan's mom. She tried to whisper in her mom's ear, but it was hard to whisper when she was crying. Her mom couldn't understand what she was trying to say.

"Could we go in Dad's office?" Katy asked. Mom took Katy's empty hand and they walked to Dad's empty office.

"What's the matter?" Mom asked again. Katy couldn't answer because now that they were by themselves she was crying harder. Mom asked if someone had hurt her, and Katy shook her head. Then slowly she opened her hand to show her mom the orange Statue of Liberty pencil topper.

"I looked!" was all Katy managed to say before she started crying again. Mom sat down and pulled Katy close, wondering what on earth could have happened to make her daughter so upset.

Katy finally managed to calm down enough to tell her mom what had happened.

"I'm really, really sorry I did it," Katy sobbed. "I know I wasn't supposed to!"

Katy's mom gave her a big hug. "Katy, I know Mrs. Large won't be upset with you, but you need to go to her and confess. You know you won't enjoy using that pencil topper if you don't tell her what you did."

"I know," Katy agreed.

"I'm glad you have such a sensitive conscience, Katy," Mom told her. "A lot of kids wouldn't think a thing about peeking to get the prize they want. It shows me that even though you did something wrong, you have an honest heart. That makes me very happy."

"Do you think Mrs. Large is still here?" Katy asked.

"Let's go see," Mom said, taking Katy's empty hand again and leading her back to the foyer.

Katy spotted Mrs. Large beside the coat rack. The knot in her stomach was getting bigger. Tears started streaming down her cheeks again. She wiped them away, but she knew there was no hiding the fact that she was crying because her face and eyes were already red.

Katy's mom tapped Mrs. Large on the shoulder and told her Katy needed to tell her something. Mrs. Large smiled and leaned forward. Katy began to speak, but Mrs. Large told her she would have to speak louder because she couldn't hear her.

"I peeked when I was getting my prize out of the mailbox," Katy said, her voice trembling. "I know I wasn't supposed to and I'm really sorry. You can have the pencil topper back." Katy held out the pencil topper in her open palm.

"That's okay," Mrs. Large told her. "You can still keep it. Thank you for telling me, though." Katy nodded. "I saw on the calendar that you and your brother and sister are doing a program for us next month," Mrs. Large said. "I'm looking forward to that!" Mrs. Large picked up her bag of puppets and turned to leave. "Good night!"

"Good night," Katy and her mom said together. It was over. Katy almost wished Mrs. Large had made her give the pencil topper back, but at the same time she was glad she got to keep it.

It was bedtime when they got home. While Anna brushed her teeth in the bathroom, Katy went into their room and closed the door. She pulled out her drawer under the bed and picked up her box. She still clutched the Statue of Liberty pencil topper in one hand. On the way home from church she had decided that she didn't really want to be reminded of cheating every time she saw it while she did her schoolwork. She decided to put it in her box instead.

"There, S.P.," she said to Sugar Plum as she dropped the pencil topper in the box. "When I see that eraser it will remind me of how it feels to cheat, which is awful, and how it feels to confess, which is hard but worth it. And it will remind me of Mrs. Large and church."

Katy thought about how she had laughed at Beth's question about the Easter bunny. She felt bad for having been part of an unhappy church memory for Beth. She hoped the Easter play would be a happy church memory they could share together.

11

Puppets and Popcorn

Katy liked the new way of doing school at their house. She still did her math and science every day and listened to her dad's history lectures after lunch twice a week. She still practiced her handwriting and tried to remember what the difference is between a verb and an adverb. They still did school, but it felt different. When their mom wrote down what they did each day in her record-keeping notebook, she didn't just write down "Math: Lesson 67" or "Language Arts: pages 55-56." She also wrote things like, "worked on script for Golden Agers puppet show" and "rehearsal for Easter play at church." Mom helped the kids see that they were really learning and experiencing important things all the time. Learning had become their lifestyle, and it was fun. Almost everything they did counted as school in one way or another.

On the day of their program for the Golden Agers, Seth, Anna, and Katy practiced their puppet show one more time before packing all their supplies in a box and heading to the church building with their mom in the brown minivan.

Katy enjoyed the potluck before the program, especially the fried chicken and Oreos. Their friend Irene made sure they each got a piece of her carrot cake.

While the adults finished their meal and cleaned up the kitchen, Seth, Anna, and Katy went behind the puppet stage to get ready. They hung up the white curtain on which Mom had drawn the outline of a tree with no leaves. They set up all their props on the floor in the order in which they would need them. Anna went around to the front to introduce their show. She had decided she could be in front of the stage for that long.

"We are going to do a puppet show for you based on Ecclesiastes 3:1-8," she said. "It's called 'There Is a Time.'"

As Anna walked back around behind the stage, one of the ladies in the audience said, "I hope she's going to talk louder than that."

"Louder, Anna!" Mom called out. Anna worked hard to speak up as she read the script. Seth was the puppeteer for the boy puppet and Katy was the puppeteer for the girl puppet.

"For everything there is a season," Anna read. She and Katy and Seth worked as quickly as they could to poke pink construction paper flowers through tiny slits in the curtain so that from the audience it looked like the tree was blossoming in springtime.

"Isn't that wonderful?" they heard Mrs. Large exclaim. It made Katy feel good to know that she liked their show already. They replaced the flowers with green construction paper leaves to represent summer. Then to represent fall they pushed the leaves all the way through the curtain so that they fell to the floor. Next Anna dropped pieces of white cotton stuffing from above the curtain onto the puppets to represent winter.

Mrs. Large spoke up again and said, "Isn't it marvelous?"

"And a time for every matter under heaven," Anna continued. Seth and Katy made their puppets appear holding a cardboard clock, then took them back down.

"A time to be born," Anna read, as Seth's puppet shook

a yellow baby rattle and Katy's held a tiny doll wrapped in a blanket, "and a time to die." Seth and Katy made their puppets reappear, each holding a handkerchief, as they made sounds of crying.

Anna continued reading through the script while the puppets acted out each verse with their various props. Everyone laughed as Seth's puppet used a fly swatter to swat the pretend fly that Katy flew around on a stick as Anna read, "A time to kill."

Katy and Seth made their puppets hold toy guns when they entered for the last verse as Anna read, "A time for war." Then they laid down their guns and made their puppets stand together as Anna read, "And a time for peace." Seth and Katy made their puppets exit for the last time and everyone in the audience clapped.

"Come on out and take a bow!" they heard their dad call. Katy went out first, followed by Anna and Seth, and they bowed together. They went back around behind the stage to clean up the mess they had made in their hurry to get the puppets and props out in time for each verse.

"That was fun," Anna said. "I'm actually kind of sad it's over."

"But now we have the Easter play to get ready for!" Katy reminded her excitedly.

As they drove away from the church building, Mom told them they would need to get their science and language arts books out when they got back home since they hadn't finished them that morning. Katy groaned.

"I thought we weren't going to have to do them today since we did the puppet show," she whined. "I thought school was supposed to be different now."

"Katy," Mom said sternly, "sometimes I do let you have a day off from your regular schoolwork to do other things, but today isn't one of those days. I'm all for doing fun things like puppet shows and letting them be part of school, but we still have to get our regular work done. No more complaining."

"Yes, ma'am," Katy replied. She felt guilty and added, "I'm sorry."

"Hey, if we hadn't done the puppet show we wouldn't have had any of Irene's carrot cake," Seth reminded her. "That's worth doing some science in the afternoon if you ask me."

After Katy finished her science and language arts, she went to the kitchen to get a drink of water. She thought about how she had been able to go to the Golden Agers program and do a puppet show. She thought about how she was about to go downstairs to make a paper mâché piñata for their family Valentine's Day party next week. She thought about how both of those fun things counted as school. She really didn't have anything to complain about, and she felt even more guilty for having whined to her mom earlier.

When she got back to the den, Mom was putting in a movie for them to watch while they worked on their craft.

"I like being homeschooled," Katy commented as *Anne of Green Gables* began to play. Mom smiled.

"I'm glad," she said. "I like homeschooling you!"

Mom had all their supplies laid out on the card table in front of the couch. Seth blew up the balloon while Anna and Katy tore the newspaper into strips and Mom mixed two parts of white glue with one part of water. They had seen *Anne of Green Gables* so many times before that it didn't matter if they missed part of it while Mom explained the paper mâché process to them. They knew what the characters in the movie were going to say, anyway.

"Seth, it's going to pop!" Anna exclaimed as Seth blew the balloon bigger and bigger.

"It has to be big," Seth told her. "It's going to be a pig. Besides, the bigger it is, the more stuff Mom can fit inside!"

They worked together to dip the newspaper strips into the mixture and lay them on the extremely large balloon. With so many hands, it didn't take long to cover it with three layers. They couldn't do any more on their project until it dried, but they stayed in the den to enjoy a little more of the movie anyway.

When Dad came home from work, he found everyone still watching *Anne of Green Gables*.

"Is it that time already?" Mom exclaimed when she saw him. "I had no idea it was that late! I'm sorry. I haven't even started supper."

"That's okay," Dad told her. "Just make sure a mouse hasn't drowned in the plum pudding sauce like it did at Green Gables!" Everyone laughed.

"That makes me think of that time at church when there was a mouse in the oven during the potluck," Anna said.

Katy shuddered. "That was nasty! I don't think I'll ever forget that smell."

"This is Thursday, isn't it?" Mom asked. "I don't know why it hadn't even occurred to me that it's family night. It's too late to do anything much for supper."

"Popcorn and cheese and crackers sounds like a family night supper to me," Dad suggested.

It didn't take long for Mom to pop the popcorn on the stove and for Anna and Katy to make a platter of cheese and crackers. They took the food to the den and went back to Prince Edward Island with *Anne of Green Gables* while they ate. After supper, Dad carried everyone back in time to the days of the Civil War as he read aloud from *Across Five Aprils*.

Later in the evening, something made Anna think of stories she had heard of when Dad worked as a DJ on the local radio station in the town where he grew up.

"Dad, can we listen to that recording you have of you as a DJ, please?" Anna begged.

"Oh . . ." Dad cringed. "You really want to?"

"Yes! Please?" Anna begged again. "DJ Jack still lives!" DJ Jack was Dad's radio name.

"Oh, all right," Dad agreed. "If I can find it."

In the third place he looked, Dad found the old cassette tape with snippets of his time as a disc jockey when he was in college. He had explained to the kids before how he changed the vinyl records to play the songs on the radio. While the songs played he tried to think of something clever to say or a joke to tell in the next break. During some breaks, he gave a weather report. Sometimes he turned those into jokes, too.

Dad put in the tape. His voice sounded so young. "It's 7:33 with DJ Jack Porter. Night falls on Columbia. *(thump)* Night just fell. Lows in the upper 60s, highs in the lower 80s. It's 74 degrees. Hang on to your eardrums!" A song began.

"You really want to listen to this?" Dad asked.

"Of course!" Anna said. "It's part of our heritage!"

The voice of their dad spoke again on the tape. "It's DJ Jack What's-His-Name! If you walk a mile in my shoes, you'll get corns just like I got! Fair tonight. Might be fine tomorrow, but it's only fair tonight." Dad looked embarrassed. Katy didn't understand many of her dad's jokes because she wasn't familiar with the songs they referred to, but she still enjoyed hearing his voice. He had obviously enjoyed his job as a DJ.

"DJ Jack is my name," the voice on the tape continued, "play it is my game." Another song began.

Dad let them listen until it was time to get ready for bed. The kids gathered up the dishes and took them back upstairs to the kitchen while Mom wrote down what they had done for school that day in her record-keeping notebook.

"Talk about a full day!" she said. "I have so much to write down. There's all the regular school, plus doing the puppet show and making a piñata for art, watching *Anne of Green Gables* and reading *Across Five Aprils*. I like days like this!"

"And don't forget about listening to DJ Jack!" Anna reminded her. "That's history, too!"

"Hey, watch it!" Dad answered, pretending to be offended at being categorized as history.

"Modern history," Anna specified with a smile. Dad laughed a good hard laugh, which made everyone feel happy deep inside.

Every now and then, Katy remembered the big argument her parents had the day she went to the Christmas party at the Lanfords' house. That day, she had wondered if their family was going to be okay, even though her parents had assured her they were. On nights like this, there wasn't a doubt in her mind.

12

A Pig and a Storm

Katy's hand began to ache as she wrote "God is Love and He Loves You!" on another index card. Anna and Katy were making valentines to take to the nursing home so the kitchen staff could put one valentine on each resident's tray at lunchtime. Seth sat at his desk, scribbling down the answers for his math lesson as fast as he could. Katy and Anna had already finished theirs.

Katy chose three heart stickers to decorate the card, just as she had each one. The stack of completed cards was getting bigger. Just after Katy reached over to make the stack a little more straight, Sparky burst into the den, dashed under the card table, and jumped on the couch, knocking over the whole stack of cards in the process.

"Sparky!" Katy cried.

"Sorry," Anna said. "He's a little extra energetic today. He's excited it's Valentine's Day."

"Yeah, right," Seth replied. He had just finished his math and was on his way to join them making cards. "He's always a little extra energetic," he said, giving Sparky's belly a rub. They picked up the cards on the floor and finished making the rest.

Katy made a special valentine for Miss Aimee, the lady from New York she had met when they went caroling at the nursing home at Christmastime. Her mom said Katy could stop by Aimee's room when they dropped off all the cards before their Valentine's Day party at church.

The employees at the nursing home appreciated the valentines when the Porters delivered them and said the residents would, too. "These will be the only valentines many of them receive," one of the nurses told them.

Katy remembered exactly where Miss Aimee's room was. Mom told Katy she could deliver the valentine by herself while they waited for her in the lobby.

Katy felt very grown up walking down the hall alone. She came to Miss Aimee's room and knocked, even though the door was open.

"May I come in?" Katy asked.

Miss Aimee looked up and beamed. "Oh! My friend is here!" she exclaimed. Katy wasn't sure Miss Aimee would remember her, but apparently she did.

"Happy Valentine's Day!" Katy said. She walked to Miss Aimee's wheelchair and handed her the valentine. Miss Aimee opened it and read the message.

"Did you make this?" she asked.

"Yes, ma'am," Katy answered, trying to speak loud enough for Miss Aimee to hear.

"I don't know when anyone made me a valentine," Miss Aimee told her. "Would you put it on my bulletin board up there?" Katy tacked up the card. She was glad Miss Aimee would be able to look at the valentine and be reminded that God is love. Katy hoped Miss Aimee would be reminded that she loved her, too.

"I'll think of you every time I see it," Miss Aimee said, as if she had been reading Katy's thoughts. Miss Aimee asked Katy why she wasn't at school.

"We homeschool," Katy told her.

"I don't blame your parents for that one bit," said Miss Aimee, "the way this world is changing."

"We're going to have a party this afternoon, just our

family," Katy told her. "We made a piñata in the shape of a pig and painted it pink. My mom filled it up with treats and things. We're going to take it to the church building where my dad works and see who can break it open!"

"You'll have fun with that," Miss Aimee said. "I wish I could watch."

"I do, too," Katy told her. "Well, I'd better go."

"Be careful out there," Miss Aimee warned. "I heard there's going to be a bad storm. Come see me again."

"I'll ask my mom to bring me soon," Katy assured her. "Bye! Happy Valentine's Day!"

"Happy Valentine's Day, my friend!" Miss Aimee called back.

The Porters picked up pizza as a special treat and drove to the church building where their dad was at work. Mom and the girls set up lunch while Dad and Seth figured out a way to suspend the pig piñata from the ceiling in the middle of the room. After the paper mâché had dried the week before, they had cut sections from a paper towel tube and taped them on the balloon to be the pig's feet and snout. They covered the open ends of the tubes with masking tape and then painted it all pink. Katy had drawn on the eyes and mouth and Anna

had made ears and a curly
tail out of pink construction
paper and taped them on.

"That's a fine looking
pig," Dad told them. The pig
dangled from the ceiling,
spinning slowly one way
and then the other until it
finally stopped.

After everyone finished
their pizza, they took turns
wearing a blindfold and swinging a baseball bat to see
who could break open the piñata. Dad managed to
whack the snout off on his first turn, but the pig didn't
actually break open until Seth's second turn when he hit
it so hard, the whole thing came crashing down from
the ceiling.

Mom had filled the pig with candy, chocolates,
pencils, erasers, and three notepads. Everything divided
evenly between the kids, plus there were three chocolates
each for Mom and Dad.

When Dad came back in from taking the pizza box
to the dumpster, he told them they needed to hurry.

"Looks like the storm the weatherman predicted is hitting sooner than he thought it would. It's sleeting out there now."

Cureton Drive was covered in ice by the time the Porters got home. Since their driveway was slightly uphill, Dad decided to park on the street. Their feet crunched through the frozen grass as they walked through the yard to the side door. As they were about to step inside, they heard a loud crack across the street and turned in time to see a huge limb fall to the ground just a few feet from their neighbors' car.

As they stood around in the kitchen, they continued to hear cracks and crashes as the weight of the ice proved too much for one branch after another. They all hoped a branch from the maple tree in the front yard wouldn't come through their roof. Suddenly everyone jumped at the sound of a terrible blast somewhere outside. At the same moment, the lights in their house went out.

"What was that?" Katy exclaimed. It sounded like a bomb had exploded somewhere.

"It must have been a transformer," Dad told her. "It's going to be okay."

"What's a transformer?" Katy asked.

"It's something that helps electricity get to our house," Mom said. "That's why the lights went out."

"It means our heat is out, too," Dad said. He gathered up some flashlights in case the power was still out when it got dark. As Dad went through the house checking pipes and putting towels on the floor behind the doors to stop any drafts, Katy and the others stood around not knowing exactly what to do. Katy could tell by her dad's face that he was worried.

"Come on to the living room, kids," Mom said. "I'll read to you. Now is it perfect or what that we're in the middle of reading *The Long Winter*?"

Even though she was under a blanket, Katy's toes grew steadily colder as Mom read about Laura Ingalls and her family facing one blizzard after another on the Dakota prairie.

Mom had planned a special meal of meatloaf, mashed potatoes, and green beans for their Valentine's Day dinner, but she couldn't cook it without electricity. Instead they had peanut butter and jelly sandwiches, chips, and bananas. They had some of their chocolate from the piñata for dessert.

Mom brought her antique oil lamp to the table so

they could eat by lamplight, but she had never actually tried to use it before. She had the flame too high and the smoke blackened the ceiling above the table. Mom quickly blew out the lamp and decided they could do just fine with flashlights.

Without electricity, everyone felt like going to bed earlier than usual. Katy thought it was exciting to brush her teeth by flashlight. Mom put extra quilts and blankets on all the beds. They hoped the power would come back on in the night and that the heat would warm up the house by morning.

It didn't.

When Katy woke up the next morning, the chilly air was biting her face. She couldn't believe how cold the room was.

"Anna? Are you awake?" Katy whispered.

"I've been awake for a long time," Anna told her. "I just don't want to get out of bed. It's freezing!"

Dad came into their room wearing his coat, hat, and gloves. "I'm sorry it's so cold, girls," he said. "Get up and get dressed. The power is on at the church building, so we're going to go spend the day over there. Mom's packing breakfast and some school books and we'll get out of this refrigerator as soon as we can." Dad left their room and closed the door. Anna looked out the window beside her top bunk.

"Whoa!" she said. "Katy you've got to come up here and see this!" Katy climbed up the ladder and peered out. Everything she could see outside was coated with ice. The ice was beautiful, but the broken tree branches and limbs scattered all over the yard and the street made it look like a tornado had gone through. Anna and Katy saw that the van was running as their dad tried to get all the ice off so they could drive it—somehow—to the church building.

The van felt extra toasty after being in the freezing house. The roads were treacherous. Katy noticed that her dad's knuckles were white from his tight grip on the steering wheel as he tried to dodge fallen limbs and keep the van from spinning on the ice. The van crept along like a snail. When they finally turned into the church parking lot, everyone breathed a big sigh of relief.

Katy knew her dad was used to being at the church building all day on a weekday, but it felt strange to her. Mom had brought the school work that was quickest and easiest to pack up, but they finished it all before lunch.

Seth, Anna, and Katy decided to explore the familiar building and look for anything new and interesting.

The afternoon was long. Dad frequently turned on the radio to get updates on areas where the power was back on. The news anchors also gave advice on how to keep warm, how to avoid food spoiling in refrigerators and freezers when there was no power, and how to stay safe on the ice if you had to get out.

By late afternoon, the power at their house was still out. Mom called the Evans, a family from church, to see if they had power. When Mrs. Evans said they did, Mom asked if they could spend the night. Katy and Anna were thrilled with the opportunity to spend the night with their friends Jenny and Rachel and their parents.

The next day was a little warmer. Even though it wasn't as cold, the Porters still had no power at their house. Workers were busy all over the city cleaning up the streets and trying to get power to everyone who had lost it.

After another day at the church building, Dad decided they would spend that night back at their own house so they could keep an eye on things. Anna and Katy were disappointed they weren't going back to the

Evans' house. They tried to make the most of the cold temperatures by playing olden days in the basement and pretending they were facing one blizzard after another like the Ingalls. Since there was no power, Seth could not work on the math game he was in the middle of programing on the computer. After their olden days game, Anna and Katy joined Seth in a game of marbles.

Finally, four days after the ice storm hit, the power came back on in the Porters' house. It was nice to hear the whirr of the refrigerator and be able to flip a switch and have something actually happen. Katy couldn't remember how many times she had flipped switches when the power was off, forgetting that it wouldn't do anything.

"Anna?" Katy asked, as the two of them brushed their teeth before bed. "Could I please sleep on the top bunk tonight? You haven't let me in a long time."

"Hmmmmm," Anna replied as she brushed her teeth. She spit in the sink. "I guess so."

"Yesss!" Katy exclaimed. When she said it, toothpaste dribbled out of her mouth and down her pajama shirt. She leaned over the sink to spit. "Why do I always do that?" she asked.

"Well, if you hadn't asked to sleep on the top bunk it wouldn't have happened," Anna teased, "so maybe that shows you just shouldn't sleep on the top bunk!"

"Anna!" Katy whined.

"I'm just kidding," Anna told her, then added, "I'm just kidding that I'm just kidding. I'm just—"

"Anna, wait!" Katy interrupted. "What's that smell?"

"Jack!" the girls heard their mom call urgently. "Something smells like it's burning."

Anna and Katy put down their toothbrushes and followed Mom down the hall to the kitchen where Dad was standing, sniffing the air and looking around. Seth had noticed the smell from his room and soon joined the rest of the family in the kitchen. The smell was strongest near the fridge. As Dad opened the door of the freezer section, clouds of black smoke began to billow out around them.

"Whoa, Nellie!" he exclaimed as he slammed the door shut. He reached around to unplug the fridge as quickly as he could.

"What happened?" Anna asked.

"There must have been a power surge," Dad said. "I sure am glad we were home."

When Katy asked why, Seth told her that power surges can start fires. That made Katy pretty nervous.

The Porters transferred the food that was upstairs into the basement freezer. Dad said they would probably have to shop for a new refrigerator the next day. Katy didn't know how much a new refrigerator cost, but she imagined it was a lot, especially since her dad sounded so depressed about it.

"Can we keep this one to play with?" Katy wanted to know. "We could move it to the basement and play house and restaurant and all kinds of things with it! Please?"

"No," Mom told her. "It wouldn't be safe to let you guys play with an old fridge. Someone might get trapped inside. Besides, there's no good place for it down there."

"You mean we have to get rid of it?" Katy asked. She didn't like things to change, even when it came to refrigerators.

"Don't be silly, Katy," Anna said. "It's a refrigerator. It's not like it's a family loom."

"I think you mean heirloom," Mom corrected her.

"Heirloom," Anna repeated. "That's what I meant."

"I still wish we could keep it," Katy said as she turned

to leave the kitchen. "Too bad it won't fit in my box," she said to herself as she walked down the hall to her room.

Katy pulled open the drawer under her bed and took out her box. She opened it and looked inside at the doll with the blue hair, the birthday cards, the certificate from the Jazzy Four, and all the other special things that lay in front of her.

"I guess it would be kind of silly to try to keep an old refrigerator," Katy said aloud. "Some things just can't fit in a box."

13

Party Guest

Katy opened the drawer under the stove to find a pot lid that would fit on her white construction paper. When she found one the right size, she traced around it on the paper, put the lid back, and returned to the den in the basement. Katy, Anna, and Seth were all working on their displays for the homeschool group's international fair.

Their mom had let each of them choose a country to learn about in preparation for the fair. They each had a list of assignments to complete for their displays, but they could do more than that list if they wanted to. They each had to make the country's flag, trace a map of the country, write a report about it, and make a chart showing the country's population, top five exports, and things like that. They were also supposed to come up with something three-dimensional for their displays.

Katy wanted to do Japan because she knew that Mrs. Large at church used to live there. She felt sure she would loan her some souvenirs for her display. At the same time, Katy thought Japan was too typical and wanted to pick a country not many people would know anything about. She asked her mom if she could do two displays.

"If you don't mind the extra work, it's fine with me," Mom had told her.

Katy didn't mind. She had flipped through the pages of her family's *Flags of the World* book, looking for a flag she liked from a country she had never heard of. She settled on Mauritius, a tiny island nation off the coast of Madagascar in the Indian Ocean.

When Katy got back to the den, Seth was working on his report about Norway and Anna was painting a scene of tulips for her display on the Netherlands. Katy put newspaper on the card table and laid her white construction paper on top. She painted the circle she had just traced red so it would look like Japan's flag. When she was finished, she divided another piece of construction paper into four equal sections to paint the flag of Mauritius. She painted the sections red, blue, yellow, and green.

Katy found out that dodo birds lived on the island of Mauritius before they became extinct. She found a picture of one and set to work to mold one out of clay.

The next Sunday evening before class, Katy went up to Mrs. Large to ask if she could borrow some of her Japanese souvenirs and told her why she needed them. Mrs. Large was delighted to say yes and told Katy she would bring some things for her on Wednesday. Katy hoped she wouldn't forget because the international fair was on Thursday.

Mrs. Large did not forget. On Wednesday she found Katy in the hall to give her the items she had brought. She invited Katy to sit down beside her so she could explain what each item was. Katy could tell she was excited to be remembering her time in Japan. Mrs. Large didn't have any children and her husband had died a long time ago.

Mrs. Large showed Katy three white circle coasters with scalloped edges, each stamped in blue with a Japanese garden design. Next she pulled out a set of four napkins, each stamped with a beautiful pattern of yellow roses with green stems and leaves. They were made of

rice paper. Katy could not imagine ever wiping her dirty mouth with one of those beautiful and delicate napkins. The last item Mrs. Large pulled out of her bag was a small white rectangular box. She opened it up and pulled out a small fan. She opened the fan to show Katy the Japanese calligraphy written on one side. On the other side was a simple painting of a tree branch with pink blossoms painted on a shiny silver background. Katy took it carefully, excited to be holding something so beautiful in her own hands.

The international fair was scheduled to begin at the Porters' church building at 11:00 Thursday morning, but everyone was supposed to arrive before then to set up their displays. There was to be a potluck at noon, and everyone was encouraged to bring international foods.

Katy was proud of the dal puri she and her mom had made the day before. Much of the traditional food of Japan included seafood, which Katy didn't like, so she had chosen to make dal puri, a traditional flatbread eaten in Mauritius. Katy liked it much better than seafood.

Katy's mom had invited Mrs. Large to come to the fair to see her Japanese souvenirs on display. Katy was excited for her to see them. When Mrs. Large arrived at Katy's table, she said, "Oh, how marvelous!" She looked at Katy's paper Japanese flag and read every word of the report Katy had written.

"Thank you for loaning me these things," Katy told her, pointing to the coasters, napkins, and fan.

"You can keep them," Mrs. Large said.

"Are you sure?" Katy asked excitedly. "Thank you!"

"I'm glad someone will be able to enjoy them," Mrs. Large told her.

The Porters walked around the fellowship hall together, looking at all the displays. When they reached the far side of the room, they stopped at Tonya Kerry's display about Scotland.

"Hi, Katy!" Tonya said. "Guess what! I'm having a birthday party on Saturday and my mom said I could invite you. Want to come? It's at 5:00. We're going to have hamburgers and hot dogs and chocolate cake."

Katy looked at her mom. "May I go?" she asked.

"I'll check with Dad," Mom answered. "I think it should be okay." Tonya and Katy looked at each other and smiled. Katy hoped her dad would say yes.

That evening, as Katy carefully placed the Japanese coasters, rice paper napkins, and fan in the special box under her bed, her mom poked her head into her room.

"Dad said it's fine for you to go to the party," Mom told her. "I called Tonya's mom to say you could come."

"Thank you!" Katy answered. She could hardly wait until Saturday.

The next day, Mom took Katy to a bookstore so she could pick out a present for Tonya. Katy knew that Tonya liked horses, so she chose *Misty of Chincoteague,* a book about wild ponies.

On Saturday evening, Mom drove Katy to the Kerrys' house. Katy held the present she had wrapped for Tonya in her lap. She hoped Tonya would like it. It always made her anxious to watch someone open the present she gave them as she wondered what they would think about it.

The Kerrys' house was much bigger and fancier than Katy's house. Tonya's dad traveled often with his work and Katy could tell that he must make a lot of money doing whatever it was he did.

The living room was decorated with pink and purple streamers. Five helium balloons in different shapes floated up above the table. Katy only knew two of the other girls who were there.

They played two party games before everyone gathered in a circle to watch Tonya open her gifts. It made Katy smile to hear Tonya squeal with delight when she saw the horse on the cover of the book Katy gave her.

Tonya's parents gave her a fancy china tea set from France. The other girls wanted to hold the different pieces as Tonya unwrapped them, but all the miniature dishes with their pink roses looked so fragile and delicate that Katy was afraid to touch them.

Before they ate their hamburgers and hot dogs, Mrs. Kerry took the tea set upstairs and put it in Tonya's room. As she came back down she told everyone that Tonya's room was off limits for the evening until they found a good place for the tea set. The table where she put it was a little wobbly.

Everyone sat on the floor in the living room to eat since there wasn't enough room at the table. When Tonya's mom went back to the kitchen to get the cake ready, Tonya told everyone about the dress her grandmother had sent her for her birthday. It sounded beautiful.

"Come on upstairs," Tonya said. "I'll show you!" Tonya jumped up and all the other girls followed her—except Katy. Katy wanted to see the dress, but she remembered that Mrs. Kerry had told them not to go in Tonya's room. Katy stayed where she was.

When Mrs. Kerry came back into the living room carrying the cake, she was surprised to see Katy by herself.

"Where did everyone else go?" she asked.

"They went to see Tonya's new dress," Katy answered.

Mrs. Kerry hurriedly put the cake down on the coffee table. "I told them not to go up there!" she said, alarmed. Just then, the group of party guests came down the stairs, laughing and smiling. Tonya walked behind everyone else, crying.

"What happened?" Mrs. Kerry asked. The other girls stopped and looked at Tonya. They hadn't even noticed she was crying.

"Someone bumped the table," Tonya wailed, "and two of the cups fell off and broke!"

Mrs. Kerry huffed and said, "I told you girls to stay out of that room!" She was not happy. Katy couldn't blame her and was extremely glad she had not gone upstairs with the others girls.

"Can you order me another tea set?" Tonya asked.

"We'll have to see," Mrs. Kerry answered. "Let's have cake."

Katy felt sorry for Tonya, having to wipe away tears and try to enjoy cake while her special birthday present lay broken on the floor upstairs. She wondered if the other girls had remembered they weren't supposed to go up there, or if they had remembered and just gone anyway.

After dinner, the girls sat around the living room, some playing games and some just talking and giggling. Two of the girls near Katy began making jokes that were not very nice. They looked at Katy, expecting her to laugh with them. Katy looked down. She didn't think the jokes were funny and she knew they shouldn't be talking that way, but she didn't know what to say.

"Oh, yeah," one of the other girls said. "Her dad's a preacher."

"I guess she's only supposed to laugh at nice jokes, then," the other girl answered. The two of them giggled more and then started whispering so Katy couldn't hear.

Katy was relieved when her mom arrived to pick her up. She thanked Tonya and Mrs. Kerry for inviting her and followed her mom to the van.

On the way home, Katy told her mom about the party, the tea set, and what the girls said toward the end.

"I'm sorry, Katy," Mom told her. "I'm proud of you for standing up for what was right."

It was nice to hear her mom say that, but Katy felt guilty for not standing up more. "I should have reminded them that we weren't supposed to go upstairs," Katy said to herself. "I should have said something to those girls about not joking like that. Instead I just sat there."

As she looked out the window of the van, she remembered the lesson Mrs. Lanford had taught in class the Sunday before about the apostle Paul. When they played Draw Your Sword, Katy had been the first one to find Acts 28:31 and she had read aloud about how Paul proclaimed Jesus "boldly and without hinderance."

"I had two chances to do that at the party and I missed them," Katy said to herself.

Katy thought about how being laughed at because she wasn't giggling at a dirty joke was about as much persecution as she had ever experienced. That wasn't really very much. She knew that Christians were persecuted and killed for their faith a long time ago and even today. If they could stand up to their persecutors and be bold for Jesus in that kind of situation, surely she could be bold for Jesus when someone laughed at her.

"God," Katy prayed silently as they turned onto Cureton Drive, "I'm sorry I was a wimp. Please help me to be brave and stand up for Jesus. I missed two perfect chances."

The next evening at church, Mr. Wade held another rehearsal in the fellowship hall for the Easter play. Katy and Anna were each playing the part of a woman who traveled with Jesus, watched Him be crucified, and went to the empty tomb after He rose from the dead. Katy's favorite line was one she said after the boy playing Jesus walked across the stage carrying a heavy wooden cross.

"What is to become of us all now?" Katy had memorized from the script. "This is the end of our hope!" She tried to sound as desperate as she could when she said the line and hoped that she could make herself look like she was crying. She hoped maybe she could make some of the people in the audience cry for real.

The play had helped Katy think hard about the amazing story of Jesus and how He really did die on the cross and come back to life. The story was new for Beth and Jackson. They had plenty of questions, which Mr. Wade tried to answer patiently. He had a tendency to use complicated words when he answered them, though, so he often didn't really help them understand things much better.

"How did Jesus get picked to be Jesus?" Beth asked Katy during rehearsal.

"Well," Katy said, wondering how to answer, "Jesus just *is* Jesus. He just *is* God's Son. He was up in heaven, then He came to earth and died for us, and then He went back to heaven." She was going to leave it at that, but she realized that Beth hadn't been hearing about Jesus all her life like she had. She realized that even though no one was threatening to take her to jail if she talked about Jesus, she could still be bold and proclaim Him right there. She decided to say more.

"Jesus loves you a whole lot, Beth. He loves everybody. He wants us all to decide to follow Him, and He wants to save us."

It wasn't many words, but it was a start. Katy hoped that Beth understood. Saying those words made Katy think about how much Jesus really loved her and how He loved Beth just exactly the same. Grungy tennis shoes don't matter to God, as long the person's heart is seeking Him.

Katy could tell Beth liked being in the play. Jackson had a hard time staying focused during rehearsals sometimes, but he had made comments that showed he was thinking hard about the story of Jesus and what it meant. Sometimes Mr. Wade or one of the other adults had to chase Jackson around the room to catch him and make him do what he was told. He wanted to do a good job and he tried, but sometimes he just didn't seem to know how to behave. Every week he mentioned that his mom promised she would come watch the performance on Good Friday.

Katy watched Beth and Jackson climb into the back of the Lanfords' car after church. Then Dad turned off the lights in the church building and locked the door. The Porters all walked out to their minivan, which was the only remaining vehicle in the parking lot.

"I'm glad Beth comes to church," Katy commented.

"I am, too," Mom said. "She's a good friend now, isn't she?"

Katy nodded and said, "It's neat to get to talk about Jesus to people who don't know much about Him. It makes me want to do it more."

As they headed home, Dad and Mom continued a discussion they had begun inside.

"So have you decided to go?" her mom asked. Katy didn't know what they were talking about.

"I'd like to," Dad replied, "but only if we all go."

"We can take school with us, and I'm sure we'll find

some field trips to take," Mom said. Katy was desperate to know what they were talking about.

"So, should we plan on it?" Dad asked.

"Let's do," Mom answered. "The kids haven't been to Michigan yet. It's another state we could color in on the map."

"Are we going to Michigan?" Katy asked.

"Yes," Mom answered. Then she turned to Dad. "Right?"

"Yes," Dad answered. "There's a minister's conference up there and we're going to make a family trip out of it."

"Where will we stay?" Katy asked.

"The church is going to pay for us to stay in a hotel," Dad answered. The Porters didn't stay in hotels very often, so this was going to be a special treat. Katy hoped there would be a swimming pool.

14

Accidents and Field Trips

The day before they were scheduled to leave on their trip to Michigan, Katy, Anna, and Seth gathered in the den to fold laundry. Mom told them they could put in a movie while they worked, as long as it didn't slow them down. There were still several items on the list of things that had to get done before the trip. Anna suggested they watch *Anne of Green Gables*, which they had started while working on the pig piñata, but had never finished.

As they folded washcloths and matched up socks, Mom came in to figure out which school books they should take and which ones they should leave at home. She didn't want to take much because she wanted to have plenty of time for field trips, but she thought it would be good to take a few things for the times they were just hanging around the hotel.

After she had gathered the books she wanted to take, Mom got lost in the world of Green Gables and temporarily forgot about the list of things to do before they left. She finally pulled herself away and headed back upstairs. Soon after she left, the kids all heard her voice call out in distress, "Oh, no!"

They all sprang to their feet and raced up the stairs to see what had happened. They found their mom in the bathroom standing on a floor covered with water. She shook her head and looked as if she might begin to cry at any moment.

"I cannot believe I did that!" she said.

"What happened?" Anna asked.

"I put a shirt in the sink to soak," she said as she grabbed a towel out of the cabinet. She sopped up as much water as she could with the towel before wringing it out over the bathtub. "When I turned the water on to fill up the sink, I told myself it was a bad idea to leave the room, but I did it anyway. I was going to come right back, but I got busy downstairs and I completely forgot about it."

"You mean the water's been running this whole time?" Katy asked.

"Yes," Mom answered. "Seth, please go get the mop from the basement. Girls, grab some towels and help me sop this up."

Before long Seth came hurrying back to the bathroom. "Mom, there's water dripping from the ceiling down there!" he told her.

"Are you serious?" Mom cried in dismay. She stepped over Anna and Katy who were down on the floor, and hurried to the basement.

"Is it bad?" Anna asked Seth.

"Well, you remember what's under us, don't you?" Seth said. "All those piles of boxes?" Anna and Katy groaned. They did remember. Katy thought about what was in all of those boxes: paperwork, scrapbooks, books they didn't have room for on the shelves in the den, and lots of other things that really shouldn't get wet. "She's going to need help down there," Seth said, as he turned to follow Mom down the stairs.

"I guess he forgot the mop," Katy said to Anna. "Should we keep doing this or go help downstairs?"

"If we don't get this water off the floor," Anna

answered, "it's just going to end up on the boxes downstairs." Katy and Anna continued to work together until the floor was as dry as they could get it. As they headed down the stairs, they met Seth coming up carrying a box.

"We have to carry everything outside and lay it out on the driveway to dry," he told them. Katy and Anna looked at each other in dismay. They had no idea the basement cleanup was going to involve so much work. They didn't have any choice but to jump right in and do what they could to make it go faster. They were thankful it was a sunny day so the boxes could dry out before they left on their trip the next morning.

When Dad got home from work a little while later, Seth was carrying the last box outside. Dad had to park on the street because the driveway was covered with boxes.

When bedtime came, Katy wanted nothing more than to crawl under her covers. She was tired. She felt bad for her parents, though. Even though she and Seth and Anna had helped with what they could, she knew her parents had a lot more to do before they could go to bed.

When Katy woke up the next morning, she found her mom in the kitchen packing their breakfast and lunch for the road. Katy offered to help.

"That would be great, Sweetie," Mom said. "You can go on and put those things that are on the counter in the cooler. I'm going to go help Dad get things loaded in the van."

Katy got to work as Mom headed out the side door. In a few minutes, Katy heard a loud noise outside. She couldn't tell what had happened. She ran to the side door and looked out. The van was partially out of the garage and Katy could see her mom in the driver's seat with her head down on the steering wheel.

"Mom?" Katy called, alarmed. "Mom, are you okay?" Mom looked up at Katy. She closed her eyes and shook her head.

"I forgot to close the passenger door before I backed out," she said through the open window of the van. "That noise you heard was the passenger door hitting the garage." Dad walked around the back of the van from the other side.

"The passenger door won't close," he said. "It's broken."

"Can we still go on our trip?" Katy wailed.

"Be quiet, Katy, and let us think," Mom answered.

"But will we still be able to go?" Katy persisted. "Can you fix it? Did we do all this work for nothing?"

"Katy, just be quiet," Mom repeated.

Katy began to ask again, "But, Mom, I just want to know if we will—"

Mom snapped back harshly in a way she had never done before. No one in their family ever talked to each other like that.

Katy closed her mouth and felt crushed. Then she realized how she had been peppering her mom with questions after her mom had told her to be quiet. She knew she owed her mom an apology, but she didn't know if she should apologize right then or not since her mom had told her to be quiet. She decided to keep her mouth closed for now. She turned back to finish packing the cooler. She felt like the trip was ruined before it had even begun.

In a few minutes, Mom came back into the kitchen.

"I'm sorry I snapped at you, Katy," Mom said.

"I forgive you," Katy answered. "I'm sorry I kept talking when you told me to be quiet."

"I forgive you," Mom told her. "I can't believe I did that. Dad asked me to go on and back the van out of the garage so we could load it. I just didn't notice that the passenger door was open."

"Will we still be able to go on our trip?" Katy asked.

"Dad wants us to go on and get loaded up and drive to the mechanic. He's hoping it will be a quick fix and then we can head to Michigan."

When everyone and everything was loaded into the van, Mom backed out of the driveway. Dad sat in the passenger seat, holding the door closed as tightly as he could. If he let go, it would swing open.

Thankfully their mechanic was just a few blocks away. When they got there, the mechanic took a look at the van and said it would take him several hours to get the door fixed. Dad wanted to be at the ministers' conference when it started that evening, so he told the mechanic they couldn't wait that long.

"I can just get it closed and you can keep it locked and not use it on your trip," the mechanic suggested. Dad decided that would be the best solution.

It took the mechanic less than thirty minutes to bend the door into place and get it closed. He locked it and put duct tape over the handle on the inside and the outside so that no one would forget and accidentally open it while they were on their trip. Dad made an appointment to get the door repaired after they got back.

Katy looked at her dad's face. He didn't look mad, but still he seemed down.

"I hope it's not too expensive," Katy heard her mom whisper to him. "I'm sorry, Jack."

"It's okay, Eva," Katy heard her dad reply as he put his arm around her mom's shoulders. "Maybe the trip isn't ruined after all," Katy said to herself.

The trip to Michigan was six hours. Katy was used to long drives since they often went to Tennessee to visit relatives. Those drives were even longer. Mom drove so that Dad could look over the conference material he had received in the mail.

Since Anna was sitting beside the cooler, it was her job to pass out the cheese, crackers, chips, and grapes they had brought for lunch. After everyone was finished, Dad surprised them all by suggesting they drive through somewhere and get milkshakes. No one turned him down. Mom got off at the next exit and found a place to order three chocolate, one vanilla, and one strawberry milkshake. She pulled out of the fast food parking lot and into the gas station next door so they could fill up the van with gas. When Dad unbuckled, Mom assured him that she could get the gas since it wouldn't be easy for him to get out.

"No, that's okay," he said. "I'll get it. And I can drive now."

"You kids have a sweet dad," Mom said.

"And a sweet mom," Dad added.

Mom got out of the van and Dad climbed over the driver's seat so he could get out. After Mom got back in and climbed over to the passenger seat, she said, "I feel like we're playing leapfrog!"

Since both cupholders were full, Dad set his milkshake carefully on the driver's seat while he pumped the gas. When the tank was full he climbed back in and sat down. He quickly sprang up out of his seat with a sudden gasp.

"Honey?" Mom exclaimed. "What is it?"

Dad had forgotten about his milkshake. It was all over the back of his pants and oozing out of the paper cup onto his seat. Anna quickly grabbed the roll of paper towels in the food box beside her.

"Here, Dad," she said, trying not to laugh. Katy felt bad for her dad, but she wanted to laugh, too. She looked back at Seth and saw that he was smiling, but trying to hide it. It was pretty funny, but at that moment their dad did not seem to think so. He cleaned himself and the seat as best he could with paper towels and sat down on a plastic bag. Katy wasn't sure if the bag was to keep his pants from getting the seat dirty or the seat from getting his pants dirty. She decided not to ask.

"I guess we'll be going to the hotel first," Dad said, pulling out of the gas station. "I wasn't sure we would have time before the conference starts, but I don't want to show up like this."

"It could be a good conversation starter!" Anna added.

"I think we'll be able to think of other things to say," Dad answered. "I'd rather not be the talk of the conference." He reached around and tickled Anna's knee.

"I think he's beginning to see the humor in the situation," Seth whispered to Anna and Katy.

"Water in the basement, a broken van door, and a smushed milkshake," Anna commented. "What next?"

"Let's hope nothing!" Mom answered.

Everyone was glad when they pulled into the hotel and it looked like Dad would have plenty of time to change clothes and get to the conference before it started. After he left, everyone else headed to the pool.

Katy hadn't been in a pool since the summer before when she took swimming lessons and didn't do well enough to earn the reward patch at the end of the season. She was determined to learn to swim better. The pool was heated and felt wonderful. Katy raced Seth back and forth across the length of it. He always won, but Katy was used to that.

As they headed back to their room, each wrapped in a towel and trying not to drip too much water on the floor, Mom stopped at the display of travel brochures to see if there were any places that looked like they would make a good field trip. She picked up a few that looked interesting and they headed back to their room.

Mom decided a nearby historic village looked like the most promising destination. The next morning, they all got in the van, dropped Dad off at the conference, and headed to Troy Historic Village.

"Are we going to do school today?" Seth asked.

"We are doing school!" Mom answered. "You don't

necessarily have to have books to 'do school.' When you look at the map to tell me where to turn, that's geography. When we get to Troy Historic Village, that will be history." Katy smiled. She liked homeschooling.

It took them the rest of the morning and into the afternoon to go through the village. Katy loved seeing the antique artifacts in one building after another. It looked like Laura Ingalls could step out of the general store or the log cabin any moment. Seth enjoyed the print shop. They all had fun sitting at the desks in the school building and writing on the chalkboard. As they played the old fashioned games set up on the lawn, Seth asked if the games counted as P.E.

"Absolutely!" Mom said.

After they checked out in the gift shop where Katy bought a pencil, Anna bought a postcard, and Mom bought an ornament for their Christmas tree, Mom asked the attendant a question.

"We're here from Illinois for my husband to attend a ministers' conference," she said. "We homeschool, so we were able to come along. Would it be possible for us to bring our school books over here tomorrow and have school in the school house?"

The lady thought for a moment. "I don't see why not," she said. "Sure, that would be fine."

"Great idea, Mom!" Katy said, as they walked down the brick sidewalk to the van. "This will be fun!"

The next morning, Seth carried the box of school books to the van when they set out for the day. They dropped off Dad at the conference again and headed back to the historic village.

Mom had finished reading them *The Long Winter* and they had moved on to *Little Town on the Prairie*. Mom carried that book and told the kids each to get their math and science books. They walked to the little

red brick school house and each chose a desk. After they finished their science, Mom told them to take turns and each sit on the stool in the corner so she could take their picture wearing the dunce cap.

"What's a dunce cap for?" Katy wanted to know.

"Naughty children had to sit in the corner and wear a dunce cap as punishment," Mom told her. "It was to make them feel ashamed." When it was Katy's turn for the stool, she crossed her arms and tried to put on a pouty face, but it was hard not to smile. The big paper cone hat on her head made her feel quite goofy.

At the end of the day, they wrote a thank you note to the village for allowing them to use the school building. Mom said Katy would be the one to write it so she could have some handwriting practice, but everyone worked together to decide what she should write.

The next day they left their schoolbooks in the hotel room and drove to the town of Frankenmuth about an hour away.

Katy enjoyed seeing the German-style buildings up and down the streets in the town. They enjoyed browsing through an enormous Christmas store, a candy store, and several other shops, including a clock shop that was shaped like a cuckoo clock. It looked very much like the cuckoo clock that hung in the Porters' living room.

As they walked down the street after their picnic lunch, Seth spotted a place called Memory Lane Arcade and asked if they could go there.

Inside the yellow building they found rows and rows of antique arcade games. Mom gave each of them some money and said they could pick the games they wanted to play. Seth spotted a game called Scientific Batting Practice and chose to play that one first. Seth controlled the batter from the mechanism on the outside of the case as the little metal baseball player figures moved around on the inside. The girls decided to watch Seth play and then find their own games so the fun would last longer. Seth successfully made the batter hit eleven out of the fifteen balls pitched to him.

Many of the games in the arcade were in beautiful wooden cases. As they walked along the rows, they realized that some of them were indecent and they had to pick and choose carefully which ones they played.

"Why do they have bad ones?" Katy wanted to know. "I didn't think they had games like this back then."

"It's easy to think that things were better a long time ago," Mom answered, "but sin has been around since the garden of Eden."

Even though they had to turn their heads at some of the games, they all had fun laughing at the funny old figures inside the machines and enjoying one game after another. Katy and Seth raced each other on a bicycle game. They each spun a wheel on the outside of the machine as fast as they could. The wheels made the bikers inside the machine race around a track. Seth won.

Katy and Anna both chose to use some of their money at a machine that engraved letters on metal tokens they could take home and keep. Anna went first. The machine engraved her shiny blue token and let it drop into a small compartment at the front of the machine. After Anna took her token out, it was Katy's turn. Katy chose the letters she wanted the machine to engrave. The machine whirred and buzzed and soon a shiny gold token clinked against the compartment door at the front. Katy opened it and read the words carefully to make sure she hadn't made any mistakes: KATY PORTER APRIL 9 AGE 9. The star shape in the middle of the token was engraved with the words: MEMORY LANE FRANKENMUTH.

That night, the Porters enjoyed one more swim in the hotel pool. Katy felt like she was getting better and wondered if she was finally a good enough swimmer to earn a patch if she took lessons again.

Mom read aloud one chapter after another from *Little Town on the Prairie* as they drove home the next day. Just after they crossed the Illinois state line, Dad noticed blue lights in his rearview mirror and pulled over onto the shoulder. The blue lights followed him.

"What happened?" Mom asked in a startled voice as she looked up from the book.

"I think I was going a little fast," Dad said. "I was distracted, thinking about how much they are going to charge to fix the van door when we get back. Now I'm wondering how much this ticket is going to be."

Dad rolled down his window as a young policeman walked up beside the van.

"Hello, sir," the policeman said to Dad. "Do you know why I pulled you over?"

"I think I was going a little fast back there," Dad admitted. "I apologize about that."

"May I see your license and insurance card?" the policeman asked. As Dad pulled his license out of his billfold and Mom found the insurance envelope in the glove box, the policeman looked at Seth, Anna, and Katy in the back of the van. He asked where they were traveling, and Dad told them they were on their way home from Michigan.

The policeman took the license and insurance card back to his vehicle. Katy asked what he was doing.

"He's looking up dad's record to make sure he's not a dangerous criminal," Anna told her. Katy wished Anna didn't always know more than she did, but she reminded herself that Anna had lived two years longer than she, so it really was understandable.

Several minutes later, the policeman came back to Dad's window and handed him the two cards. "I'm going to let you go this time," he said, "but I'll ask you to keep your speed down as you go through the small towns."

"Yes, sir. Thank you," Dad replied.

"Have a good trip!" the policeman told them.

When he was gone, Dad gave a big sigh of relief.

"Kids, you should a learn a lesson from that," Mom told them. "Your dad could have been angry and given excuses, but instead he was calm and respectful.

"Maybe since he didn't give you a ticket," Anna said from the back, "we have enough money for milkshakes!"

"Too dangerous," Dad replied. "Someone might sit on theirs." Everyone laughed, even Dad.

When they got home, Mom got out her record-keeping notebook which she had accidentally left at home and asked for help remembering everything she should write from their trip. Even though they had only used a few of the books they took, the different subject categories in the notebook filled up fast as they remembered all the things they had done on their trip.

Before she climbed onto the bottom bunk that night, Katy pulled out the drawer under her bed so she could put in the gold token from the arcade in Frankenmuth. Katy looked at all her treasures in the box from their first year of homeschooling. It had been a good year. She was surprised that it was almost over. She wondered if she would have any more treasures to put in her box before their summer break began.

15

Hope

On Saturday, the day after the Porters returned from
their trip, Dad and Seth worked on reorganizing
the boxes in the basement that had gotten wet when
the sink overflowed. Mom, Anna, and Katy drove to
the church building to help with a costume work day.
There was just one week left before Good Friday and the
performance of the Easter play. Katy didn't know what
she would be able to do to help with the costumes, but
she hoped there would be something.

When the Porters arrived, several sewing machines
were already humming in the fellowship hall as ladies
sewed costume pieces together. Some other ladies
stood at tables cutting out more costumes, belts, and
headdresses. Mom set up her sewing machine at an

empty table and apologized for being late. She explained that they had just returned from their trip the evening before.

In a few short hours, all the remaining costumes for the play were finished. Katy had been given the job of making a name tag for each person in the play. Mrs. Lanford helped her know which costume was for which person. Katy pinned the correct name tag on each one so all the kids could easily find their costumes when it was time to perform the play.

On Sunday evening, Anna and Katy headed to the fellowship hall together for the last rehearsal before Friday's performance. As soon she walked in, Katy saw Beth sitting in the back row of chairs by herself with her arms crossed and a sullen expression on her face. Katy sat down beside her. Jackson was bouncing off the walls. Mr. Wade had a hard time keeping him under control. Katy overheard two of the adults who were there to help with the rehearsal talking behind her. They thought they were whispering, but Katy could hear them plainly.

"I wonder what's been going on at their house," one of them said, looking at Jackson.

"There's no telling," the other one replied. Her voice

sounded as if she was rolling her eyes as she talked. Katy hoped Beth had not overheard them, too.

It had taken Katy a while to realize that Beth and Jackson couldn't have known how to behave in church because they weren't used to being in one, but she realized it now. Katy wished people wouldn't make comments that would make Beth and Jackson feel different from the rest of the kids.

After Beth and Jackson started coming to church, Katy often felt proud of the fact that she knew how to act just right at church so that she never got in trouble with her teachers. She felt proud of the fact that she knew the answers to most of the questions in class. She felt proud that she could find verses quickly in her Bible. Then one Sunday, Dad preached a sermon about how much the Bible has to say about pride and how bad it is and how much God hates it. Katy realized that her pride was much worse than Jackson climbing over the seats and certainly worse than Beth wearing grungy tennis shoes that didn't match her dress to church.

When the time came during rehearsal for Katy's favorite line, she tried to imagine that the seats were full of people as she said loudly, slowly, and clearly with as much emotion as she could manage, "What is to become of us all now? This is the end of our hope!"

During the dress rehearsal, Katy managed to remember all of her lines except one. Mr. Wade had to prompt her on that one. The rehearsal was full of other mistakes and mishaps. Mr. Wade kept running his fingers through his hair in frustration.

Katy remembered hearing her Granddaddy Wes talk about dress rehearsals. He had been in several plays before Katy was born. Katy had always been fascinated by the black and white photograph of her granddaddy dressed up like one of Robin Hood's merry men. Granddaddy Wes always liked to say that a bad dress rehearsal meant a good performance. Katy sure hoped he was right.

On Friday morning when Katy got up, she could already feel butterflies of excitement inside her at the thought of performing the play that night. As she and Anna headed out of their room for breakfast, they found two pieces of paper taped to their door, one for each of them. One said Anna Porter across the top and the other said Katy Porter. Each one had a big star printed in the middle.

"What are these for?" Katy asked.

"In theaters the famous actors have stars on their dressing room doors with their names on them," Anna said. "I bet Dad made these."

Katy ran on to the kitchen where her dad was pulling a pan out of the oven.

"Did you put the signs on our door?" Katy asked.

"Well, I thought the stars of the play needed stars on their door!" Dad replied. Katy gave him a hug.

"Thanks, Dad," she said. Then she noticed what was in the pan her dad was holding. "Pull-apart coffee cake!" she exclaimed. "Yum!"

"Only the best for the stars!" Dad told her. Katy

smiled as she picked up the stack of plates and the pile of forks beside the sink and took them to the table.

Katy tried to concentrate on her math and science and spelling that morning, but her mind kept wandering to the performance that was getting closer all the time. After lunch she went over the script to study her lines and make sure she remembered all her cues.

The Porters ate an early supper so they could be at the church building by 5:30. As they loaded up, Mom started to climb over the driver's seat to get to her seat, but Dad reminded her that the passenger door was fixed now and she didn't have to.

"I got so used to getting in this way!" Mom said with a smile, continuing to climb over. "It's kind of fun. I'll use my door to get out at church."

The play was scheduled to begin at 7:00. Mr. Wade had encouraged everyone to invite people who weren't a part of their church to the performance. Katy had invited Chinway's family and Tonya's family. She hoped at least one of them would come.

Mom and a few other ladies tried to keep everyone calm and quiet as they tied on belts and positioned headdresses in a crowded classroom. All the kids were excited, except Jackson. Mrs. Lanford had picked up him and Beth and brought them to the church building. Their mom had told them she would be there to watch the performance, but she wasn't there yet.

"Our mama said she'd come, but she ain't here," Jackson said, when one of the ladies asked why he was upset. He refused to put on his costume and said he didn't want to be in the play. Katy decided to see if she could help.

"Come on, Jackson," she said gently. "We need you! If you're not in the play, who is going to say your lines?" Jackson stared straight ahead with his arms folded. Katy tried again. "You've done a really good job when we've practiced. Don't you want to put your costume on? It's almost time for it to start."

"I ain't gonna be in it," Jackson said. He didn't sound like there was any way he was going to change his mind.

Katy wished she knew how to convince him. She thought about how her dad had put a sign on her door that morning and made pull-apart coffee cake for breakfast because it was a special day. She wished Jackson had someone to do things like that for him. Whitney came over and stood beside Katy.

"I really wish you would do your part, Jackson," Whitney said. "The play will be better if you're in it."

"I ain't gonna be in it," Jackson insisted. Then he muttered, "She promised she'd come."

Even though Jackson could be frustrating and hard to handle sometimes, everyone loved him. Jackson had a good heart and was so lovable under the prickles that showed up sometimes. Katy had seen him hug Mrs. Lanford and her mom and the other ladies many times. It was obvious that he loved coming to church. Everyone wanted him to succeed and everyone knew that he could if he had the chance.

It was almost 7:00 when someone accidentally stepped on Megan's costume and the seam on one side ripped open.

"It's okay!" Mom assured her. "I'll go get some safety pins, and everything will be fine." When Katy's mom opened the door to go get the pins, Katy caught sight of a woman sitting on the back row of the auditorium. The woman looked a bit uncomfortable and Katy could tell she felt out of place. Katy looked at her face and noticed a strong resemblance to Beth.

"Jackson, come look!" Katy whispered. "I think your

mom's here!" Jackson perked up and hurried over to the door. He peeked out and turned around with a big grin on his face. Katy knew she must have been right.

Jackson hurried over to the other side of the room where his costume lay in a wadded heap where he had thrown it down. He put it on as quickly as he could. It was wrinkled, but that didn't matter. He was ready to do his part. Mom came back in and pinned Megan's ripped seam back together.

The auditorium was nicely filled. The first time Katy went out for a scene, she scanned the audience. Her parents were sitting together two rows from the front. She didn't see Chinway's family, but Tonya and her mom were there.

The play ran smoothly. Finally the time came for the scene when Katy said her favorite line. She went out on cue with all the rest of the kids who were supposed to be in the crowd.

They stood along the back of the stage and Colin, the boy playing Jesus, entered carrying a wooden cross. The cross looked heavy. Colin carried it with the top part over his shoulder and the other end dragging along the floor. He walked across the front of the stage slowly, stumbling now and then on purpose, but making it look so real. His agonizing groans sounded genuine. Katy saw several people in the audience wipe their eyes.

Colin wore a crown of twisted thorns on his head. The thorns were positioned so that they wouldn't really poke him, but as Katy stood in her spot looking at Colin, she thought about how the thorns on Jesus' crown really did dig into his skin. The blood on Colin's face and costume was just a mixture of ketchup and water, but Jesus' blood was real.

As Colin passed, Katy fell to her knees as she had practiced so many times. She buried her face in her hands and pretended to sob. She held her eyes wide open behind her cupped hands to try and make them

water. She peeked through a slit between her fingers to make sure Colin had passed before she picked up her head and said in an agonized voice, "What is to become of us all now? This is the end of our hope!" Katy buried her head in her hands again and the lights went down to end the scene.

Katy and her friends from church continued to act out the Easter story. When they finished the last scene, they all gathered together to bow while the audience clapped.

After the play was over, Katy saw Beth and Jackson run to their mom and give her a big hug. They all looked so happy together. Katy was glad their mom had seen and heard the story of Jesus that night. She wondered if she had heard it before.

Mr. Battle made a point to find Katy after the play was over. Instead of pinching her cheek like he usually did, he put his arm around her shoulders and told her she did a good job. Katy smiled and thanked him. "You looked like you were really crying up there!" he said. Katy smiled again.

Tonya and her mom thanked Katy for inviting them and said they enjoyed it. As other people complimented her and said she did a good job, Katy smiled so much her cheeks got sore. She liked being an actress.

After Katy got ready for bed that night, she went and found her mom on the couch in the living room. Katy felt like snuggling, so she curled up beside her mom. Mom was on the phone with Shirley Conner. After a few minutes, Katy's mom said,

"Well, Shirley, I better go. I think Katy's ready for me to tell her goodnight." A little bit later, Mom tried again. "It was good to talk to you, Shirley, but I better—" Her voice trailed off and she looked at Katy and mouthed the word, "Sorry!" Katy didn't really mind getting to stay up a little bit longer.

Finally Mom said kindly, but firmly, "Shirley, I'm going to have to say goodnight. Okay. I'll talk to you soon. Yes, I'm sure we can. Bye." Mom hung up the phone and sighed. "Now," she said to Katy, "is there something you need?"

"I just feel like snuggling," Katy said. Mom hugged her close. "I'm glad Jackson was in the play after all. He did a good job."

"He sure did," Mom agreed. "He's a sweet little boy. He has a lot to learn, but he has a good heart."

"I'm glad he started coming to church," said Katy. "I'm glad we've been able to show him Jesus."

"I am, too, Katy," her mom said. "And I'm glad we were able to show Jesus to their mom. It was special that she came. I know it meant a lot to her kids."

"You know that line I had in the play where I said, 'This is the end of our hope'?" Katy asked. Mom nodded. "Do you think their mom has hope?"

"She might not think she has hope," Mom told her, "but everyone who follows Jesus can have hope no matter what."

"I hope she learns that," Katy said. She yawned and snuggled in closer to her mom. She was glad her parents had taught her about Jesus.

After a few moments of silence, Mom gave Katy a kiss on the top of her head and told her she better go to bed. Katy forced herself to get up off the couch. She stretched and walked sleepily down the hall to her room. She stopped briefly to look at the signs her dad had put on their bedroom door that morning. It felt so nice to be loved.

16

Katy's Lip

On Saturday, the day before Easter, the Evans family came to the Porters' house for dinner and a Bible study. Anna and Katy talked with Jenny and Rachel about the fun they had being in the play and how much they hoped Mr. Wade would write another one sometime.

"I was so nervous," said Jenny, "but it was really fun."

"I hope I can have more lines next time," Katy said.

"Colin sure did a good job playing Jesus," Mrs. Evans joined in. "I think half the auditorium was crying when he carried that cross. He was good."

After dinner, everyone sat around in the living room and Dad led a Bible study. Anna held Sparky in her lap. Sparky was nervous with the Evans in the room, and didn't run wild all over the place as he usually did.

Dad talked about the story in the Bible of the two men who met Jesus on the road to Emmaus after the resurrection. They sang two songs and then Mr. Evans led a prayer.

When the Bible study was over, Katy walked across the room to Anna and asked if she could hold Sparky. Anna didn't mind, so Katy tried to pick him up out of her lap. Sparky was still nervous about their guests and didn't want anything to do with Katy. He growled at her, and sat rigid in Anna's lap.

Katy didn't want the Evans to think that Sparky didn't like her, so she said casually, "Oh, Sparky," and tried to pick him up again. Sparky growled more fiercely and snapped in Katy's face. He managed to get her bottom lip between his teeth.

Katy cried out in pain and surprise. Anna gasped and said, "Katy, are you okay? I'm so sorry!" Anna gave Sparky's snout a smack. Mom hurried across the room to Katy as she told Anna to go put Sparky in his kennel.

Katy's lip was throbbing. Dad rushed to get a cold rag for her to put on the bite. Katy sat trembling while her parents looked closely at her lip and talked about whether or not they should go to the emergency room.

"What do you think?" Katy's mom asked Mrs. Evans. "Do you think she needs stitches?" Katy didn't like everyone staring at her. She was embarrassed. Her lip hurt. She was upset with herself for trying to pick up Sparky a second time after he gave his warning growl. Katy didn't want to pull the rag off her lip so that Mrs. Evans could see it, but her mom made her do it anyway.

"That's pretty deep," Mrs. Evans said. "I would definitely have someone look at it right away."

Dad picked up the phone and called Dr. Gaines, a physician in their church. When he got off the phone, he said that Dr. Gaines had offered to meet them at his office so they wouldn't have to go to the emergency room.

Katy and her parents got ready as quickly as they could and headed to Dr. Gaines' office. The Evans offered to stay at the Porters' house with Seth and Anna until they got back. Katy wished that she could be playing games with them instead of going to the doctor's office.

They pulled into the parking lot just behind Dr. Gaines. It felt strange to walk into a dark and deserted doctor's office on a Saturday night. Dr. Gaines turned on the lights in the waiting room and then in the hall. He led them into the first exam room and told Katy to climb up on the table. He gently pulled her hands and the rag away from her lip.

"Yeah, that's a good bite," he said, " but I'll have you stitched up in no time." Katy's stomach churned. She didn't want stitches.

Dr. Gaines began to gather the supplies he needed. "I usually have a nurse here to do all this," he said. "I hope I can remember where everything is."

"Katy, do you remember the last time you got stitches?" her mom asked. Katy nodded and almost smiled. That story had become a family legend. Her mom told Dr. Gaines the story. "Katy had a mole removed from her back when she was six. I can still see her lying facedown on that exam table. A nurse and I both had to hold her down. Just as the doctor was about to give her the shot to numb the area, Katy cried out, 'Just a minute! Just a minute! Just a minute! Just a minute!' He pulled back and she was crying and kicking, not wanting that needle to touch her! I don't remember how many times he started to give her that shot and every time he got close she would cry, 'Just a minute! Just a minute! Just a minute! Just a minute!' He finally just went ahead and gave her the shot anyway." Dr. Gaines laughed. "We've teased Katy about that a lot, haven't we, Katy?" Mom asked. Katy nodded, smiling.

"Well, I don't have a nurse here to help hold you down, so just don't do that this time!" Dr. Gaines teased.

"I won't," Katy said. She hoped Dr. Gaines knew she was too grown up to act like that now.

Dr. Gaines opened a syringe package and Katy knew it must be the shot to numb her lip. As he held the needle close to her lip, Katy desperately wanted to cry, "Just a minute! Just a minute! Just a minute! Just a minute!" but she didn't. She closed her eyes and tried to relax. She felt the poke and her eyes brimmed with tears. Before long, her lower lip felt as if it was slowly inflating like a balloon.

While they waited for her lip to get completely numb, Katy's parents and Dr. Gaines chatted about this and that. Katy lay still with her eyes closed. After a few minutes, Dr. Gaines checked to see if Katy could feel him touch her lip. She couldn't.

Dr. Gaines picked up a needle threaded with black thread. He leaned over Katy, studied her lip carefully, and began to sew. Katy couldn't feel the needle going in, but she could feel the gentle tug of the thread as he made the tiny stitches.

When it was all over, Katy and her parents thanked Dr. Gaines and headed out to the van while he stayed to clean up the exam room.

"Don't we have to pay anything?" Katy asked.

"He'll have his office send us a bill next week," her dad told her.

"I hope it's not too expensive," Katy said. Dad put his arm around her.

"Don't you worry about that," he told her. "You're worth every penny. And whatever it costs, I assure you it will be much less than a trip to the emergency room would have been."

"He sure was nice to meet us over here," said Mom.

"Did he do that because you're the preacher?" Katy asked.

"Well, that and because we're friends," her dad answered.

"I guess being a preacher's family has its rewards," Katy said. Her parents laughed.

It was late, but not too late for a milkshake. Dad said that a good patient deserved a prize. He turned into

the parking lot of a fast food restaurant and pulled up to the drive-through.

"Do the parents of a good patient get a prize, too?" Mom asked.

"This one certainly does," Dad answered, pointing to himself. "So that means you get one, too!" Dad ordered a cookie dough shake for Katy, a peanut butter one for Mom, and a chocolate one for himself. Katy sipped hers slowly. Her lip was still partially numb and felt funny around the straw.

Katy was still drinking her milkshake when they turned onto Cureton Drive.

"We should have gotten a treat for everyone at home," Mom said, "but I guess it's too late for that now."

"Why should they get a treat?" Katy wanted to know, half joking. "They didn't have to get a shot in the lip!" The anesthetic was wearing off, but her lip still felt strange when she tried to talk.

"Oh, so that's what you guys have been doing all this time!" Anna teased when she saw Katy come in with her milkshake. "I want to get stitches, too!"

"No, you don't," Katy said with a smile. "I earned every sip of this!"

"She was a very good patient," Mom praised. "Much better than the last time she had to get stitches!"

"You mean she didn't tell Dr. Gaines to wait 'Just a minute! Just a minute! Just a minute! Just a minute!'?" Seth asked.

"No, I didn't," Katy told him. "I took it standing up."

"Actually lying down," Dad corrected with a smile.

"I'm really sorry Sparky bit your lip, Katy," Anna said.

Katy held up her cup. "At least I got a milkshake out of the deal," she said. Everyone laughed.

The Evans quickly gathered their things so they could get home and get to bed so they would be ready for Easter Sunday.

It was quite late when Anna and Katy climbed into their bunk beds that night. Katy was worn out. Once her head touched the pillow, she was asleep in no time.

The next morning, everyone was in a hurry as usual

since it was Sunday. Katy ate breakfast slowly, though, afraid she might accidentally stab her lip with her fork. Her lip didn't hurt anymore, but it was strange just knowing the stitches were there.

Katy tried not to touch her lip at church, but it was hard not to when it was constantly on her mind. She kept pushing her tongue against the inside of her lip, wondering if she could feel the stitches on the other side. Mr. Battle didn't notice her stitches and started to pinch her cheek, but this time Katy pulled away.

"Please don't pinch me this time!" Katy said. "I have stitches on my lip."

"Oooo-weee," Mr. Battle said. "How'd you manage to do that?" Katy told him what happened and he said, "I reckon you'll listen next time he growls at you." Katy assured him she would.

That afternoon, Katy decided to climb the maple tree in the front yard. She wanted to be alone for a little while. Sometimes on holidays, she liked to have a little special time to talk with God.

"God," Katy prayed out loud, "thank you for sending Jesus and letting Him die for us. That must have been really hard to watch Him die on the cross. Thank you for bringing Him back to life. I really had fun doing the play. I'd like to be in more plays sometime. I'm glad Jackson was in it. Thanks for bringing his mom there. Please help her to be a good mom. Thanks for putting me in this family. And thanks that we get to homeschool. I hope I can homeschool my kids someday."

17

Room for More

"My friend is here!" Miss Aimee exclaimed when she saw Katy standing in the doorway of her room. Mom had brought Katy to the nursing home so she could see Miss Aimee on her birthday.

"Happy Birthday!" Katy said with a smile as she entered the room.

"How did you know it's my birthday?" Miss Aimee asked.

"I asked one of the nurses about it last time I was here," Katy told her. Miss Aimee invited them to sit down on her bed.

"I used to get excited about birthdays," Miss Aimee said, "but not anymore. It's just like any other day." Miss Aimee's words made Katy feel sad. She was glad that she and her mom were there to make Miss Aimee's day a little more special.

"Has your summer break started?" Miss Aimee asked Katy.

"Almost!" Katy told her. "Tomorrow is our last day of school!"

"I know you're excited about that," Miss Aimee said.

Katy nodded. "Yes, ma'am, but I do like school. My mom is a good teacher." Katy unzipped the backpack she had brought with her. "I brought you a present!" she said, as she pulled out a package wrapped in pink floral paper. "Happy birthday!"

Miss Aimee opened her mouth wide in surprise. "For me?" she said.

"For you!" Katy told her. When Katy found out a few weeks before that Miss Aimee's birthday was coming up, she decided to make her something special. She had asked her mom if they could make a little quilt together. Mom and Katy had gone to a fabric store to get the supplies. Katy chose a fabric panel that had a cuddly teddy bear printed in the middle. The teddy bear held a stuffed panda that reminded Katy of the toy panda her dad had played with when he was a little boy. Katy choose a coordinating fabric for the back. She and her mom sewed the front and back pieces together with quilt batting in the middle. Mom showed Katy how to measure and tie pieces of string all over the quilt to hold the layers in place. Katy knew the panel was probably intended to be a baby blanket, but she knew it was just the right size for Miss Aimee to have over her lap when she sat in her wheelchair. The teddy bear didn't look babyish. It just looked cuddly and sweet, and Katy thought Miss Aimee would like it.

She did. When Miss Aimee opened the gift, she didn't say a word, but the smile that spread across her face and the light in her eyes said more than any words. She gently rubbed her hand over the teddy bear.

"We made it just for you!" Katy told her.

"You made it?" Miss Aimee asked. "It's beautiful! Just look at that bear. He looks like a good friend." Katy helped Miss Aimee spread the quilt over her lap.

Katy's mom soon looked at the clock and told Katy it was time to go. They needed to pick up Dad from work and get home for family night.

"I hope you have a happy birthday," Katy told Miss Aimee. She gave her a hug.

"Thank you for the quilt," Miss Aimee said as they were leaving. "I'll treasure it. My daughter is coming to visit me tonight. I'll show it to her."

"That was a sweet idea to make the quilt, Katy," Mom told her as they walked down the hall together. "And you know it counted as school, don't you?" Katy smiled. Of course she did. Her mom had taught her to look at everything as school! "Measuring and cutting the fabric: math. Sewing the quilt: art. Visiting Miss Aimee: character. That's the most important part."

Mom had left Anna at home with instructions on how to finish the Chicago-style pizza so it would be ready for family night when they got back.

Dad decided that family night would be a game night. Everyone could pick a game for them all to play together. Katy got to go first since she was the youngest. She chose her favorite card game: Nertz. Even though she was the youngest, she beat everyone else.

Dad took off work for the last day of school. After breakfast, they all gathered in the den. Dad led a devotional about the importance of wisdom. Mom turned through her school records notebook and reminded them all of some of the highlights of the year. Everyone agreed the first year of homeschooling had been a success. It was not without its downs, but it also had plenty of ups. Everyone looked forward to a summer break, but everyone also looked forward to starting another year of homeschooling in the fall.

Seth, Anna, and Katy listened to their dad praise their mom for the good job she had done as their teacher. He opened his Bible to Proverbs 31, which talks about a woman of noble character. "This is your mother," he said as he began to read. "She opens her mouth in wisdom, and the teaching of kindness is on her tongue. She looks well to the ways of her household, and does not eat the bread of idleness. Her children rise up and bless her; her husband also, and he praises her, saying: 'Many daughters have done nobly, but you excel them all.'"

"Thank you, honey," Mom said.

Seth stood up. "I rise up and bless you!" he said. Anna and Katy stood up, too.

"You guys are the best," Mom told them. "It's been fun, hasn't it?" They all agreed that it had.

"I'm glad you can say that now," Anna said. "Did you know Katy accidentally overheard you two talking one night when Dad said, 'There has got to be an easier way to educate these children!'?"

"Well, there was an easier way!" Dad said.

"We're all learning together how to do this," Mom added. "That's what's so cool about homeschooling— learning together."

Dad reached over to the bookshelf nearest him and pulled off a stack of three papers. "I have something for each of you," he said, looking at Seth, Anna, and Katy. "After Jesus was baptized and again after He was transfigured on the mountain, God spoke from heaven. He said that Jesus was His beloved Son and that He was well-pleased with Him. I want each of you to know that I love you and that I am well-pleased with you."

Dad read the words on the paper he had for Seth, then handed it to him. He did the same for Anna. Then it was Katy's turn. Her dad looked her in the eyes and said with sincerity the words printed on the paper.

Katy,
  You are my precious daughter,
      whom I love.
  In you I am well-pleased.

                    Love,
                    Dad

All of the papers were the same except for their names and whether they said son or daughter.

Katy thanked her dad as she looked at the fancy letters he had printed on the paper for her. His words felt so good.

The Porters took a picnic lunch to a nearby park. They took some old bread from the freezer to feed the ducks at the lake. They rented paddle boats and Mom and the girls raced Dad and Seth from one side of the lake to the other. The boys won. It wasn't really fair since the girl boat had three people on it and the boy boat only had two, but it didn't matter.

Soon after they got home that afternoon, the phone rang. It was for Katy. Katy hardly ever got a phone call,

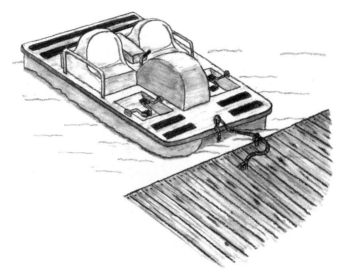

so she was surprised when her mom handed her the phone. It was Miss Aimee's daughter.

"Are you the sweet girl who made my mother a quilt for her birthday?" the lady asked.

"Yes, ma'am," Katy answered. The lady on the other end was obviously fighting back tears.

"Thank you," she managed to say. "You have no idea what it meant to my mother, or what it means to me. Thank you."

"You're welcome," Katy said. "She's a special friend."

"Well, you're a special friend to her," the lady

answered. "I just wanted you to know how much I appreciate it. Good bye."

"Good bye," Katy said. Katy hung up the phone. "How in the world did she get our number?" she asked her mom.

"The nursing home called here this morning," Mom told her. "They asked if they could give our number to Miss Aimee's daughter, and I said yes."

"She wanted to thank me for the quilt," Katy said. "She was crying."

"It means a lot to people when we show them they are loved," Mom said.

In the hustle of getting out the door for the picnic, Katy had left the paper from her dad on the dining room table. She picked it up and carried it down the hall to her room. She was glad that Anna was outside with Sparky so she could have the room to herself. She gently closed the door behind her and sat down beside the bed. She pulled out her drawer and lifted out her box. She opened it up.

On top was the paper with the star which her dad had taped to the door the day of the Easter play. She took it out and looked down at everything else. She decided to take all the items out so she could arrange them better to keep things from getting bent. She put the painting of the grassy field which she had painted a few years before on the bottom. She could paint so much better than that now. Next she put in all the flat things: the certificate from the Jazzy Four, the letter from the First Lady, the photograph with Irene, the birthday cards from her parents and grandparents, and the paper with the star. Next she carefully laid the paper her dad had given her that morning. She read the words again. Her mom was right. It does mean a lot when people show others they are loved.

On top of the papers, Katy placed the first journal she had ever completed and the purple ribbon she won in the poster contest. She put in the heart-shaped rock  she had found on vacation when she was six and the pink hairbow her mom had made for her. She put the little doll with the blue hair on one side of the box and the Japanese fan, coasters, and rice paper napkins on the other. She dropped in the Statue of Liberty pencil topper, the tangled necklace that spelled her name, the acorn, and the token from the arcade in Frankenmuth. Katy didn't mind anymore that the old refrigerator didn't fit in the box. She knew she had been silly to want to keep that.

It made Katy feel good to look at the things in her box. She liked to remember why each item was special to her. She began to think about other special things that she couldn't put in the box like feelings and memories. She decided that she needed to be keeping two boxes: one under the bed and one in her heart.

In her heart were memories such as the Christmas party at the Lanfords' house and her family's Christmas Eve talent show. The box in her heart held her special friendships with Irene and Miss Aimee and experiences of sharing Jesus with Beth and Jackson. It held the love she had for her parents and Seth and Anna. It held the love she knew they had for her.

Katy put her cardboard box back in the drawer and pushed the drawer back under her bed. Now that she had thought of the box in her heart, she couldn't stop thinking of the memories and feelings and people that were inside it.

Katy was glad there was still plenty of room for more—in both boxes.

Author's Note

The story of Katy is based on memories of my own childhood. Most of the events that Seth, Anna, and Katy experienced in their first year of homeschooling are closely based on experiences my brother John, my sister Bethany, and I experienced throughout our years of homeschooling together. My family started out homeschooling the hard way, trying to make school like the public school we had known before. It took several years for us to figure out how to relax and let homeschooling be a lifestyle, but we got there eventually. I am thankful that my parents, Ray and Charlene Notgrass, made the decision and the sacrifices to homeschool us. I had a great childhood, and I feel richly blessed.

Now I'm a homeschool mom myself. I am excited to be making memories with my husband and children as we enjoy our own homeschooling adventure.

Wherever your homeschool adventure takes you, just make sure you enjoy the ride!

Mary Evelyn

Also available from
Notgrass History:

Katy

Katy Porter is enjoying her summer break from school, climbing trees, playing with her sister, and riding bikes with her brother. One day her parents tell her they are thinking about homeschooling in the fall. Katy likes being an average girl. Will being homeschooled make her too different from everyone else? Is being different okay?

A pure story of strong character, simple faith, and a loving family.